Scattered Flowers

An Appalachia-Inspired
Short Story Collection

**Jan-Carol
Publishing, Inc**

"every story needs a book"

D1300755

Scattered Flowers
An Appalachia-Inspired
Short Story Collection

Published June 2021
Mountain Girl Press
Imprint of Jan-Carol Publishing, Inc
Copyright © 2021 Jan-Carol Publishing
Cover Photo: © Max_play / Adobe Stock

ISBN: 978-1-954978-10-2
Library of Congress Control Number: 2021940530

You may contact the publisher:
Jan-Carol Publishing, Inc.
PO Box 701
Johnson City, TN 37605
publisher@jancarolpublishing.com
www.jancarolpublishing.com

This is dedicated to all the talented authors for their participation in this collection of short stories, and to all the readers of Jan-Carol Publishing's books.

Table of Contents

A Love of Daisies   1
Jan Howery

As the Crow Flies   12
Linda Hudson Hoagland

Charlotte's Amethyst Experience   19
Betty Kossick

The Fallacious Life of Sadie Pringle   30
Rebecca Elswick

Fawn   42
Courtnee Turner Hoyle

FHB   52
Lynda A. Holmes

Help Me   57
Linda Hudson Hoagland

Marathon of Hope   63
Courtnee Turner Hoyle

Red Snow   75
Linda Hudson Hoagland

The Sixth April   83
Lori Byington

Jerome Believed   92
Linda Hudson Hoagland

Where You Are   100
Rebecca Williams Spindler

Scattered Flowers

A Love of Daisies

Jan Howery

(Around early 1900s)

Hurley Mae sat in the last pew in the back of the little white country church and watched the unmarried, handsome preacher deliver his hellfire-and-brimstone sermon. Her mind was not on his sermon, and she wasn't listening to his words. She became deaf to them as she watched his every gesture and saw him as a man, not a man of the cloth. *Wonder how he would treat a woman in bed?* she thought. *What would his kisses be like? Would he be gentle and kind, or would he blaze through lovemaking like one of his sermons?*

Twenty-one-year-old Hurley Mae had been pushed into a marriage at the early age of sixteen. Her parents had realized her beauty attracted older men, and they had seen marriage as a way to get her out of the house so they wouldn't have another mouth to feed. She was the oldest of eight children, all of them her half-brothers and half-sisters. The family had struggled. Times were not easy. Hurley Mae had dropped out of the one-room school to help with the farm and her siblings. But it hadn't been enough. The only thing left for

1

her to do had been to...get married.

But being married wasn't what she thought it would be.

Clyde Russell, her husband, was twenty years her senior. He was well respected in the town and was considered to be well-off, especially financially. He owned a small hardware store in the community, and everyone knew his name. The townspeople believed he traveled out of town on business often, but there were things that the townspeople did not know about him. He loved gambling and women. He disappeared for weeks at a time and resurfaced when he needed to rest, or when he was looking for a punching bag. Clyde physically abused Hurley Mae, often hitting, slapping, and kicking her. That was why Hurley Mae always wore dark make-up, sometimes a little too much. One of the perks of being married to a wealthy man was that she could afford makeup.

"Shall we gather for a song?" Preacher Jacob Barnwell asked, interrupting her thoughts.

The singing started, and the donation plate passed from person to person. The plate was passed through the congregation, and Hurley Mae was holding it when the song ended. She stared at the coins and dollar bills, wondering how much money was there. *I could just sneak out the door with this money and run away, but where would I go?* she thought.

"Please stand for the blessing," Preacher Barnwell instructed the congregation as he walked to the church house's front door. All stood for the blessing, and by the time the prayer had ended and a loud "amen" had echoed through the church, Preacher Barnwell was standing at the door to give goodbye blessings to his congregation.

Hurley Mae was the first at the door, and she handed him the donation plate. He smiled and took the plate, then placed it in the corner of the doorway. He reached out to shake her hand and said, "So nice to see you, Mrs. Russell. Where is Mr. Russell today?" *What a strong handshake and nice hands*, Hurley Mae thought. "Mr. Russell is out of town. He travels a lot," she answered.

"Did you walk to church today?" Preacher Barnwell asked.

Before Hurley Mae could answer, a member of the congregation pushed her aside and grabbed the preacher's hand to shake it. "Great service, Preacher. Really enjoyed it."

Hurley Mae turned away and walked down the steps of the church to start her journey home. She lived less than a mile from the church and always walked when Clyde was out of town. Clyde was one of the few who owned a gas-powered car, but she didn't like the car. Most of the townsfolk still traveled by horse and buggy, especially to the church, but Hurley Mae enjoyed her walks.

* * *

"Mrs. Russell! Mrs. Russell, do you need a ride?" Preacher Barnwell was nearing her in his horse and buggy. "I'd be happy to give you a ride. It looks like rain."

"Well, I suppose so. I'm going to stop by and see my momma. I told her that I'd stop by for dinner after church," Hurley Mae answered.

"Well, it's along the way," Preacher Barnwell said. "And I'd appreciate the company." He quickly jumped down from the buggy, walked over to her side, took her hand, and helped her step up on the buggy's sideboard. *His touch is so soft and warm*, she thought. Once she was seated, Preacher Barnwell hopped in the buggy, took the reins, and yelled a "Gitty up" to the horse.

Hurley Mae could not help but notice his striking smile, his strong cheekbones, and his soft brown eyes. *Why, he isn't much older than me*, she thought.

"I appreciate the ride," Hurley Mae said, trying to make conversation.

"It's my pleasure. Have you always lived 'round here?" Preacher Barnwell asked.

"Yes," Hurley Mae answered. "These Appalachian Mountains are my home."

"Yes, I love the mountains. My hometown is about twenty miles north of here. I have family there," Preacher Barnwell said.

Family? Hurley Mae thought. He must be married. "Family?" she slyly asked.

"Yes, six brothers and two sisters. My mother and father have since passed. They died a year apart. Mother went to be with the Lord first. Dad seemed to give up on living when she died. He died shortly after. After their passing, I had a burden to follow God's calling and..."

Hurley Mae was not engaged in the conversation. She was not listening; she was looking at his board shoulders and watching his full lips move as he spoke. *What a nicely shaped mouth*, she thought.

"...found my way here. Forgive me. I must be boring you," Preacher Barnwell said.

Hurley Mae felt embarrassed by her thoughts. "No, you're not boring me," she said with a smile.

"Do your mother and father live in the white house 'round the curve up on the hill?" Preacher Barnwell asked.

"Yes. That's homeplace. Mother and Daddy—actually, my stepdad—and my seven siblings," Hurley Mae said.

They both smiled at each other at the thought of so many siblings.

"Oh look! Look at those daisies beside the road. Do you mind stopping? I want to pick them for Mother," Hurley Mae said. "She loves daisies!"

Preacher Barnwell stopped the buggy. "Wait right there! I'll be happy to get the daisies for you!" He quickly jumped down, and in a few short minutes, he was back with a handful of bright, colorful daisies. "How interesting that those daisies are growing alongside the road, and they're so tall," he commented as he handed the flowers to her.

"Thank you. How kind of you!" Hurley Mae said.

They continued traveling down the road, making small talk along the way. They rounded the curve and started up the narrow road that led to the house on the hill. The horse snorted as he pulled the buggy up the hill.

Hurley Mae's mother pushed open the screen door and said, "I thought I heard a horse."

"Yes, Momma. This is Preacher Barnwell. You remember him, don't you?" Hurley Mae asked. "Preacher Barnwell, this is my momma, Mrs. Grayson."

"Why, of course I do. Hello, Preacher Barnwell. It's always good to see you," Mrs. Grayson said.

"He offered me a ride, Momma," Hurley Mae said as Preacher Barnwell helped her step out of the buggy.

"Well, it does look like rain," her mother said. "We're just gettin' ready to sit down for dinner. Would you like to join us, Preacher? All I need to do is set another plate."

Hurley Mae looked at Preacher Barnwell, a look of longing in her eyes. *Please say yes*, she thought.

"Are you sure it won't be a bother, Mrs. Grayson?" Preacher Barnwell asked.

"Of course not! Please join us!" she answered. "And call me Ma Grayson. Everyone else does."

"Oh, Momma, here are some of your favorite flowers, daisies. Aren't these beautiful?" Hurley Mae asked.

"Yes! Where did you find these? Alongside the road? They're beautiful! I'll set 'em on the table," Ma Grayson said as the three of them walked inside the house.

* * *

"Ma Grayson, that was the best meal I've had in a long time," Preacher Barnwell said.

"Thank you, and please feel free to join us anytime," Ma Grayson said.

"Mrs. Russell, do you need a ride home?" Preacher Barnwell asked.

"Thank you, but no. I'm staying here for a while to help Mother with some things, but thank you again," Hurley Mae said.

"You're welcome. I hope to see you again...at church," Preacher Barnwell said, bidding them a farewell.

From the front door, Hurley Mae and her mother waved goodbye as Preacher Barnwell guided his horse and buggy down the dirt road.

"How about a cup of coffee and another bite of pie?" Hurley Mae asked. "I want to talk to you about something, Momma."

"Sure. Pa, go out for a walk and take the kids with you. Hurley Mae and I want to have woman talk," her mother said to her pa.

Hurley Mae and her mother sat down at the kitchen table and sipped their coffee, and then her mother asked, "What's wrong, honey? Is it Clyde? What's he done now?"

"Momma, he's mean to me. I'm tired of being hit and beat all the time. I lost a baby," Hurley Mae said sadly.

Hurley Mae's mother stared at her and asked, "What do you mean, you lost a baby?"

"Momma, I was pregnant. Not too far along. He hit me in the stomach...over and over and over. I lost the baby," Hurley Mae said through tears. "It was for the best. I'm goin' to leave him, Momma."

Her mother sat and stared at the daisies on the table, and for a few minutes neither of them spoke. The silence was broken when her mother said, "He should be pushing up daisies for hurting you. He's like my first husband. He was no good. Abusive. When he left this world, all I had was you. I was lucky to have met Pa. He's been like a dad to you. But, Hurley Mae, you can't move back home. You have to do somethin', but movin' back here isn't the answer."

Disappointed, Hurley Mae fought back the tears. *Where am I going to go?* she thought. *I have nowhere to run to.*

"Your pa and I want you to be happy, but we barely get by now. Can you get a job?" her mother asked.

Hurley Mae choked back the tears and said, "I'll try, Momma, but I just wanted you to know that I can't stand it any longer. After five years, it's still not a marriage. I've tried. Clyde comes home long enough to beat me and force me into the bedroom with him, and then he's gone for weeks at a time. I don't love him. He doesn't love me, either, or he wouldn't treat me the way he does."

"Well, let me think about it. You know that Pa would kill Clyde if he found out what he's done to you and the baby," her mother said. "Is Clyde back in town now?"

"Well, he's supposed to be back later this evening," Hurley Mae answered. "Guess I'd better head on home before he gets there. He'll be real upset if I'm not there when he gets home."

"Hurley Mae, have you put back any money?" her mother asked. "And does Clyde have a will?"

"I've put back about five hundred dollars. He has so much money, Momma, but he'd kill me if he knew that I had that. And he's never talked to me about a will," Hurley Mae said.

"Well, see if you can sneak a little more money back, Hurley Mae. You're goin' to need it," her mother suggested.

"Okay, Momma. I've got to run. He'll be home soon," Hurley Mae said.

* * *

Hurley Mae had been home for about an hour before Clyde arrived. He came home with his usual flowers, gifts, and apologizes.

"Honey, I've missed you," Clyde declared as he poured himself a strong whiskey. "What's for supper?"

Hurley Mae tried to be very polite, but she knew that after a few drinks, he would start an argument and she would end up defending herself against his brutality. "I was planning to cook your favorites, steak and potatoes," she answered.

"Sounds great, honey! You know I hate to leave you so much, but I'm only home for a few days this time. I need you to wash my clothes, get me unpacked, and pack me up to leave," Clyde said.

"How long will you be gone this time?" Hurley Mae asked.

"Six weeks," Clyde answered as he swallowed another drink.

"Six weeks? That's a long time, Clyde," Hurley Mae said. "Can I go with you on these trips? I get lonely here without you."

"No, and hell no!" Clyde yelled. "I'm not home for an hour, and you're already on my ass for traveling. You like the gifts, don't ya? That's how you live like a queen! Ungrateful bitch!" He was hurling himself toward Hurley Mae when there was a knock at the front door. He stopped in his tracks. "Who's that?"

"I don't know," answered Hurley Mae. "I have no idea."

"Well, answer the door, bitch," Clyde snapped as he poured himself another drink.

Hurley Mae slowly opened the door. To her surprise, it was her mother.

"Finally! Hello, and hello there, Clyde! I've got to talk to you!" Hurley's mother said with excitement, pushing through the front doorway.

Clyde turned around and asked, "What! You come in my house without an invitation, and you want to talk to me?"

"Sure do! I'm here to see ya," she said. "And Hurley Mae, fix this man somethin' to eat! He and I have business to talk about. Pa and I've come into some money, and you're the man to invest it for us!"

"Money?" Clyde asked.

"Yes! Money! Three thousand dollars!" she said. "And I whipped up some tea for ya! Here, sit down, and bring me a glass, Hurley Mae."

"Momma, Clyde has a drink. He's drinking whiskey," Hurley Mae answered, moving to get a fresh glass from the kitchen. "And where did you get three thousand dollars?"

Ma Grayson ignored Hurley Mae's question, instead saying, "Whiskey? This tea has a better kick to it! It's homemade moonshine. Now, don't tell me, Clyde, that ya don't want a good drink with a good kick to it."

"Pour it up and talk to me," Clyde said. "And Hurley Mae, get to fixin' supper. Now, tell me more about this three thousand dollars."

Ma Grayson took the glass from Hurley Mae, poured the moonshine in, and dropped a small white cube into the drink. It appeared to be the size of a very small ice cube.

"What's that?" Clyde asked, looking at the drink and downing it in one big swallow.

"It adds to the kick of the drink," Ma Grayson answered. "It's the secret to white lightning."

"It's got an unusual taste to it," Clyde said. "Now, that's what I call a drink!" He sat down in his armchair and leaned back, and Ma Grayson poured him another drink as he said, "So, you got three thousand dollars, and you want me to invest it for you? How did you come by this money? Ah hell, doesn't matter. You've come to the... to the...right..."

Clyde's words trailed off, and there was silence. His eyes closed. He dropped his glass, and it shattered on the floor. Ma Grayson just looked at him.

Hurley Mae heard the glass hit the floor, and she ran from the kitchen to the living room. "Momma! Momma! What's wrong with Clyde?" she asked. She stood in shock as she stared at Clyde.

"Well," Ma Grayson said calmly, "I'm pretty sure he's dead."

"Dead?!!" Hurley Mae yelled. "Momma, he can't be!"

"Oh yes, he can be," her mother answered. "He'll never hit you again."

"What did you give him?" Hurley Mae asked.

"My special brew," her mother answered calmly. "And I spiced it up with a few drops of Aconitum roots."

"Momma, what are we goin' to do here? What are we goin' to do with him? He's dead!" Hurley Mae cried. "We're murderers!"

"Hurley Mae, get ahold of yourself. He's dead, but everyone will think that he's on a long trip. He just won't be coming back from this trip," Ma Grayson said with a snicker.

They both stood and stared at Clyde's dead body, not saying a word for several minutes.

Silence was broken when Hurley Mae slowly asked, "Momma, do ya have a plan?"

"We're goin' to dig a flower garden in the yard. Go to the shed and grab a couple of shovels, a burlap sack, and a pick," Ma Grayson ordered Hurley Mae.

Within a few minutes, Hurley Mae returned with picks, shovels, and a burlap sack.

"Where do you want a flower bed?" Ma Grayson asked. "How 'bout right in the middle of the yard? We need to get started."

"Momma, are ya sure we can do this?" Hurley Mae asked.

"Yes. Come on. We gotta start digging. It needs to be deep and long," Ma Grayson said.

Hurley Mae and her mother dug for hours in the yard. It was dark, and light rain was falling. Only two small lanterns provided light.

After hours of silence, Hurley Mae asked her mother, "Doesn't Daddy expect you home tonight?"

"No. I told him that ya needed some help with bakin' pies and that I was stayin' over," her mother answered. "Well, this looks good."

"What's next?" Hurley Mae asked.

"We'll drag him out, drop him in, cover him with dirt, put down the burlap sack, and then cover that with dirt. And then we plant the seeds," her mother said.

"What seeds?" Hurley Mae asked.

"Flower seeds," her mother answered.

"What kind of flower seeds?" Hurley Mae asked.

"Daisies," her mother answered. "Like the ones alongside the road."

* * *

After church on Sunday, Preacher Barnwell offered Hurley Mae a ride home again. When they arrived at her house, she politely invited him to come inside for pie and coffee.

"Yes, I think that I'll come in and have that cup of coffee and a piece of pie. Mrs. Russell, you sure do have a beautiful front yard. Those daisies are beautiful. How do you get them to grow so tall?"

"I have a lot of help pushing them up," Hurley Mae answered with a smile. "Call me Hurley Mae, and I hope you like date pie."

As the Crow Flies

Linda Hudson Hoagland

No service. Not even one bar. The battery was dead anyway. It was still daytime, but the sky was overcast and perfectly dull, so there was no way to tell what time of day it was, much less which direction was north or south—or anything else, for that matter. A two-lane black-top road snaked up into the distance and disappeared into some trees—or a forest, if you wanted to get technical about it. It also snaked down toward some lumpy hills and disappeared there, as well. What sounded like a two-stroke chainsaw could be heard in the distance, but it was impossible to tell whether it was up in the forest or down in the lumpy hills. This had been happening more often lately. Two different ways to go, with a dead battery, no bars, and nobody left to blame.

Ellen wouldn't be in this predicament if she hadn't gotten mad at her husband and taken off driving like a maniac, burning rubber, spinning tires, not caring who she ran into or where she was going. All she had wanted to do was get out of there, no matter where the road led her and her vintage El Dorado. She realized she would be seen as unreasonable by those who didn't have to live with her husband. Her question to each of them would be, "What would you do if your loved one of ten years told you he was getting a little bit on the side from your best friend?" He had laughed strangely after he uttered that confession, which made her wonder if he was telling the truth or just yanking her chain.

Ellen knew she had to calm down, but that was easier said than done. She kept driving, but tried to drive a bit closer to the speed limit. She had no destination in mind. The act of driving was having a calming effect on her, which was what she really needed.

On and on she drove, not realizing she was leaving civilization and entering a world unknown to her: the Stillwell National Forest. It was located about ten miles outside of the town of Stillwell. It was as if she had entered a foreign country. Her mind was rambling on, trying to find a solution to her husband-and-best-friend problem. She was not paying attention to the fact that the sun was rapidly disappearing, dropping down behind the canopy of trees.

A person was walking on the side of the road. It didn't look like one of the Appalachian Trail hikers, so she slowed down to get a good look. She nearly ran off the side of the road when she recognized the person walking. "It's Bethany, and I need to talk with her," Ellen mumbled as she raced ahead of Bethany and pulled her El Dorado onto the berm.

Ellen climbed out of her car and placed a hand on each hip, showing her contempt and defiance. Bethany seemed to recognize the challenge and scrambled to the other side of the road to avoid the inevitable confrontation. Based on the stance that Ellen had assumed, Bethany most likely knew she was in for a vicious tongue lashing, maybe even a body thrashing. Ellen crossed the road. She was going to force the confrontation. She had to have an answer for why her best friend would do something so cruel. Never in all of the years she had known Bethany would she have expected something like this to cause a rift between them.

"Bethany, just tell me why you would stab me in the back like this. I thought we would be friends forever and ever, but you seem to have a totally different idea. I really want to know why you let this happen."

"Just calm down, Ellen. It's not what you think. I am not trying to take your husband. I promise you that. This has all been a big mistake. If you must know, I don't want anything to do with Arnie."

"Then why did he tell me he was getting a little bit on the side from you? You, of all people in my world. Who should I believe, you or him? This is kind of ridiculous, don't you think?" said Ellen.

Ellen started stepping closer and closer to her, which was not a good thing for Bethany. Bethany backed up an inch at a time, trying to stay more than an arm's length away from Ellen's reach.

A vehicle drove toward both of them, so they each moved off of the pavement and out of harm's way. But it kept coming at them even though they had moved as close to the edge of the road as possible.

"Hey, you idiot, stop it! Back off! What is your problem?" shouted Ellen as, once again, her anger increased. She moved back, but she couldn't go much farther without falling down the side of the steep mountain.

"Ellen, are you all right?" screamed Bethany. She, too, was running for cover that couldn't be found. "What is happening? Why is that stupid fool trying to kill us? And that is exactly what he is trying to do!"

"Climb over the guardrail. If he wants to hit us, he will have to ram the rail really hard. That would cause some damage to his vehicle. Too much damage, I think. Or maybe I should say that I hope it will," said Ellen. "He might even go over the edge and down the mountain."

They scrambled over the rail, hanging on as tight as they could to keep from falling down the mountain, but the vehicle kept coming at them.

Ellen strained her eyes, trying to see who was driving so dangerously. "Can you see the person driving?" she screamed at Bethany, who was also hanging on to the guardrail for dear life. "The windows are tinted so dark that I can't tell if it is a man or a woman."

The vehicle came to a dead stop before it collided with the guardrail. It backed up, turned its wheels, and drove away, to the astonishment of both ladies. The vehicle's bumper had only been inches away from damaging both vehicles and both ladies.

"What just happened? Why did the vehicle go on without finishing us off, and why were they trying to hurt us? What did we do to deserve this kind of treatment?" asked Bethany as she pulled herself up and over the guardrail.

"To my knowledge, I haven't done anything bad except get mad at my husband because of you. I didn't know that was a crime punishable by death. Have you done anything that would cause this type of deadly punishment?" asked Ellen.

"Of course not, and that thing with Arnie is not what you think. If you will stay calm, I will tell you what happened. You're not going to like what I have to say, but I do have to tell you," said Bethany.

"Well, go ahead. Let me hear what you have to say. I don't have to believe a word of it, but I'll give you a chance, before God and me, to try and convince me that what you are telling me is the truth," said Ellen.

"I have never had intimate relations with your husband, nor do I ever want to do so. As a matter of fact, he isn't my friend, but you are, I hope. I saw him one day when he was being harassed by a couple of thugs. He was standing outside a restaurant on Main Street as I was walking by, and he threw his arm around me and said I was his lover."

"Why would he do that? Why did you let him do that? Who were the thugs? Why were they harassing him? I have a ton of questions that need to be answered, so you need to start answering them one at a time," demanded Ellen.

"Okay, I'll start with why he did that. It was because he didn't want anyone to bother you. He loves you that much. He was trying to throw the danger off of you and onto me and himself," said Bethany as she stared directly into Ellen's eyes.

"Okay, now tell me why you would allow him to put you in danger if you have no love connection with Arnie. I certainly wouldn't want him to do that to me, and I am married to him," said Ellen.

"Let me go on with answering your first set of questions. You wanted to know who they were. As far as I can figure, Arnie is a gambler, and he owes quite a bit of money to those guys. Did you know he gambled?" asked Bethany.

"I knew he took care of the sports pools at his place of employment, but that is the only gambling that I know of. Where is he placing bets that could cause so much trouble for the two of us?" asked Ellen.

"You wanted to know why I would allow him to do this to me. I will tell you that all I wanted to do was protect you, just like he did. I had no idea it would be dangerous for either one of us. We didn't want you put in harm's way," explained Bethany.

"Look, that vehicle is coming back. Let's go jump into my car and see if we can get away from this menace. I think they're planning to finish the job, which means one or both of us will be eliminated," said Ellen.

Bethany and Ellen scrambled to take cover within the big, heavy Cadillac El Dorado. It would take a fast-moving vehicle to shove them over the mountain. Ellen was hoping that wouldn't be possible since the other driver would be taking a chance on going over with them.

"Oh my God. Here they come!" screamed Bethany as she jumped inside the car, scooting over the bench seat to the passenger side as Ellen followed her.

Ellen pressed the button on the door to lock it after the door slammed.

"Start the car. Let's get out of here. They are getting closer and taking aim at us."

Ellen turned the key, and nothing happened. She offered up a silent prayer, and again she tried to start the car. Nothing happened. "The battery must be dead," she mumbled as she grabbed her cell phone to call for help. "No bars. Do you have a cell phone, Bethany? Call nine-one-one if you can," she said as she glanced up and saw a big black crow cruising near the windshield. "Aren't crows supposed to be bad luck?"

"Yeah. I think I read somewhere that the sighting of one crow means bad luck for some strange reason. I just hope we see more of them forming a group. According to the superstition, the luck would change to good."

"I'm not going to worry about the crows. We have trouble driving right at us," said Ellen, and they were jarred into a frightening reality when the vehicle rammed their car from the rear. "I guess they want to kill us but not go over the mountain themselves."

"They're backing up so they can do it again," screamed Bethany as she crouched down under the dashboard so she could avoid any flying glass or possible bullets headed her way. She drew her body up into a fetal position so she would be as small as possible.

The ramming stopped, and they both popped their heads up to see what was going to happen next. They saw headlights coming toward them from the opposite direction. Their assassin had driven away. They didn't move from their positions under the dashboard for what seemed like forever. They were afraid to reveal themselves completely.

"There is someone else headed this way, but the crazy SUV is gone, I think," stammered Ellen. "Can you see who is driving the newly arrived vehicle? Maybe it is a forest ranger. We could really use his help to get out of here."

The vehicle was an SUV and was driven by a forest ranger, and it stopped exactly in the center of the narrow, paved road, blocking the traffic that was suddenly coming out of nowhere. People were parking their cars around the El Dorado and getting out.

"Step back, folks. I need to speak with these young ladies," shouted the ranger as he forced the growing sightseeing crowd to back away from the badly beaten El Dorado. He walked over to the driver's side and motioned for Ellen to get out of the car. "What happened here? We have arrested a couple of men in a large SUV, a black one that had quite a bit of front-end damage. Are you the reason for that damage? Were they trying to cause your vehicle and you to tumble down the mountain?"

Ellen crawled out from her hiding space and gratefully placed her feet firmly on the ground. Bethany followed her across the front seat and got out, and they both stood leaning against the car for support, weak from fright and the loss of adrenaline.

"I think they were trying to kill us so they could use our deaths as a warning to my husband, who has reneged on his gambling debts. At least, that's what I've been told by Bethany, my best friend," Ellen said as she pointed to Bethany.

"You ladies need to go to the sheriff's office and give a statement about what has taken place today. Do you think you will be able to start your car and drive it, or should I call you a tow truck?" asked the ranger.

"Just give me a jump-start. My battery is dead. Once we get the car started, we can go far enough for me to call my husband and tell him to meet us at the sheriff's office. I'm sure they will want to talk with him," Ellen said. She wanted to plug in her cell phone as soon as the engine turned over.

Ellen and Bethany made their way through the crowd and back to the El Dorado. As they approached it, a crow flew directly over their heads and landed on the hood, then looked at them. They stood some distance away and watched the crow watching them. Another crow flew directly overhead and landed beside it. The first crow squawked, and then both flew away. They watched the crows disappear, looked at each other, and then got in the El Dorado. Only one way to go now, this time with five bars and a full battery.

Charlotte's Amethyst Experience

Betty Kossick

A brilliant early-September-morning sun puts on a bright show as a shiny blue helicopter sets down on a small, flat area that has been cleared away at the side of a chiseled Arizona mountainside in the Matazanal mountain range. The panoramic scene makes everyone catch their breath.

Charlotte's excitement increases. Satisfied that she'd found sturdy jeans, a long-sleeved My Country Girl blouse, and short boot-style footwear for the Four Peaks Amethyst Mine tour, she feels as ready as she possibly can be to enter the mine. As demurely as possible, she disembarks from the helicopter as the pilot assists her. She already knows that the mine tour will allow her to chip away with a screwdriver in order to acquire her very own mined cache of amethyst.

Four other passengers hop gingerly from the chopper. All of them—a tall, good-looking fellow named Jett, who is thirty-four;

Denny, who is nineteen; David and Mary, a newlywed couple in their mid-twenties; and Charlotte, who is twenty-six—had traveled across the country, from Atlanta to Phoenix, on a small, sixteen-passenger luxury coach that was on its maiden run. A jovial van driver named Oscar had driven them the forty-six miles north to Fountain Hills for "The Amethyst Experience." The other ten passengers who had traveled with them on the Experience Destinations coach had remained in Phoenix, where Jack, the coach driver, was giving them an all-day sightseeing tour.

The mine's guide, Mike, hands everyone a hardhat, a flashlight, and a screwdriver. All are prepared with their own Ziploc bags, ready for the mini-mining dig. The mine's small size surprises them all, and the beautiful sight of the raw gemstones captivates the five travelers, who were each drawn to the trip because of their interest in amethyst.

As Charlotte excitedly chips off pieces of amethyst after receiving some direction from Mike, she almost coos with her soft southern accent, saying, "Honey, I really did it. I mined my own amethyst!" Clutching the small stones to her chest, she announces, "I'll save this for when my prince charming comes along. Whoever he is, he can get it made into a mighty fine engagement ring for me."

She has barely said the words when the tall fellow named Jett remarks, "I think I'll save mine for when my charming princess shows up."

Momentarily, she recalls what he'd said on the coach trip out to Phoenix, when they had talked about their professions: *"Perhaps we're star-crossed artists."*

None of the novice miners leave the mine empty-handed; they each carry out some of "The Amethyst Experience." After everyone gets their fill of smartphone selfies and more serious pictures of the mine, including some of their friendly guide and the magnificent Arizona scene outside the mine, they board the chopper for Fountain Hills and Sami's Fine Jewelry, where the group will tour a store

20

filled with cut and polished amethyst gemstones, some of the finest in the world.

* * *

The nine-day cross-country trip had found Charlotte and Jett in conversation after they were seated side-by-side. At the outset of the trip, when their coach driver, Jack, called out the travelers' names alphabetically during boarding, Charlotte was first due to her surname of Clark, while Jett—"Jettson Clarke"—was second. Jack jokingly said, "Clark with a pigtailed 'e.'" They discovered that they're both Georgians with deep Appalachian family roots and that they're both of English and Irish decent, with him having more Irish roots and her having more English. However, they surmised there were no family ties in recent history. They discovered that they live fifty miles apart, with him living in Alpharetta and her living in Smyrna.

During the trip west, their happy laughter revealed that they were enjoying each other's company. Jack overheard their chatter. His romantic nature made him think, *A blooming romance? She is a pretty thing with her blond hair and green eyes, and she seems as sweet and refreshing as a cool glass of Georgia's sweet iced tea. This trip should be very interesting...*

Early in their conversations, Jett discovered Charlotte's frugal nature. She told Jett, "My parents drummed frugality into my brain. 'Debt makes you a slave.' So I watch my nickels. I'm determined to pay off my college loans, so this is my first vacation since I started teaching. I settled for this coach tour because it's more doable financially than it would be to fly off for eighteen days, even if it is via a fancy, albeit very comfortable, bus that includes some specialty dining. Jack promises to make everything satisfactory for us. I ate lots of PB-and-J sandwiches to save for this trip. Teaching high school art classes doesn't exactly make me rich. It's the mine that made me decide on this trip. 'The Amethyst Experience.' Yes, it cost five hundred dollars extra for the helicopter transportation, and it meant passing up the sightseeing in Phoenix, but I'm mighty delighted."

"Are those dusty little stones worth the spending, Charlotte?" Jett teased. He enjoyed watching her green eyes widen.

"Absolutely! I figure that it's my once-in-a-lifetime thrill. It's something I'll tell my grandkids about someday. And we'll still get to dine in Phoenix this evening. Jack made reservations for us at the Kai/Sheraton. Jack says the view is as perfect as the cuisine.

"I'll take my 'dusty little stones' home and have jewelers in Atlanta prepare them. When I was in college, I earned a nice check from Alpha-Omega Jewelers for creating a series of amethyst pastels for their showroom. I enjoyed doing that assignment so much because I felt that I was creating in a way that I hadn't before, like Adam when he named all the animals at the beginning of time. God is such an artist with all His fantastic creations. And then He allows us to be creative, too. That's when I fell in love with the beauty of amethyst and learned of the gem's assorted colors, and I thought that I'd love to own such a gem someday because it's an investment. It's also when I learned about this particular kind of amethyst; it has purple hues with flashes of red that show off under natural light. Siberian Red, they call it. I'm not for wearing showy bangles, but something like the amethyst, when cut, is beautiful artistry. To actually be here enjoying this experience is very meaningful to me."

As soon as Jett discovered that Charlotte is an art teacher, he felt camaraderie. He told Charlotte that he's an artist with acclaimed shows at the Hope Gallery in New York City, but that it's his avocation, not his profession. He felt, after realizing her frugal nature, that if she found out he earns a hefty salary, she might not be interested in getting better acquainted, or perhaps it could be the opposite, with her being much, much too interested because he is rich.

Jett is in his mid-thirties and is second in command at Deepwell Petroleum, which has offices in Atlanta. Jett has never ridden a city bus in his life, and only a few times in college had he gone on school bus excursions. He chose the coach tour because he's tired of the corporate life. Tired of spending half his life in airports. Tired of the rat race. He feels like he's never allowed to be himself. He's found life lonely at the top. No time to even date. Creating pottery and painting are his only outlets.

Jett chose to take a two-month break, a vacation that was long overdue, and not tell anyone how or where he planned to travel. He knew that he'd have to be available by phone in case of major emergencies, but he laid out his need to be left alone otherwise. He and the company's owner/president, Max Brownwyn, clashed about his extended vacation time before Jett left. The last words he heard from his close work partner of the past five years were, "You're our most valued employee, Jett, but even you can be replaced."

* * *

Now, Jett looks at his small dig of mined gems and decides that Charlotte outdid him. "I didn't do near as well as you, Charlotte. I went on various gemstone digs during archeology excursions when I was in college. I already have some raw stones. Would you like my little cache to add to yours?"

Jett's offer troubles Charlotte. She asks, "Doesn't your dig mean anything to you? Don't you want to save it? Don't you realize that these unpolished stones will soon reveal their purple magnificence? Do you have any of these already? Remember that this place is the only place in the world, except the Ural Mountains of Russia, where you can find these lovely gemstones. Didn't you see the luminous purple cast, even in the darkness of the mine, as we shined our flashlights on the vein? Surely, you want to see them cut and polished."

"Whoa, Charlotte! Remember, I told you that this mine is why I came, too. I studied gemstones in college because of my mom. She cherished amethyst gemstones. I came for 'The Amethyst Experience' in her memory. She'd have loved it and would have had the same excitement you do. But since I don't have a promised bride to give them to, I'd still like to see them cut and polished for someone who'll appreciate them. And that someone might remember me." He handed his Ziploc bag to her. "You'll show them to me all shined up, won't you?"

Charlotte abruptly turns her head away and looks out across the mountain terrain. She doesn't answer Jett. She makes no remarks about the spectacular view. Silence. But she takes his Ziploc bag and tucks it into her belly pack, along with hers. She reflects on his words from a few days before: *"Perhaps we're star-crossed artists."* And she knows. He'd meant artist lovers. She thinks, *It's only been a few days. How can this be? We need time.* Then she offers a mental prayer: *"Dear Lord, I want You to choose my mate for me. If Jett is to be my future, please show me."*

When the chopper lands back in Fountain Hills, Oscar is waiting to chauffeur the five of them to Sami's. Jett offers his hand to help Charlotte out of the chopper. She allows him to assist her. The two haven't exchanged a word since he asked her if she'd show him the polished gemstones.

"Did I upset you?" Jett inquires, his dark-blue eyes looking intently at her.

She lowers her eyes. "No, I'm fine," she denies.

Jett, of course, knows better. As he studies her, he knows he doesn't want their friendship to end with the coach tour. He thinks, *Is this how it feels to find the one?*

* * *

The next morning, at 7:30 sharp, the coach is loaded, and Jack straightens his company-emblazoned sports jacket, stretches his neck, clears his throat, and calls out to his passengers, "We're on the road back to Atlanta, but there's a lot of beautiful country to see between here and there. By the time we arrive back where we started, we'll have driven about thirty-two hundred miles."

Denny keeps teasing the passengers who took the Phoenix tour instead of "The Amethyst Experience," telling them how much they missed. David and Mary, the newlyweds, cheer him on and tell everyone about how they've arranged for Sami's to make their digs into brooches for their mothers for next spring's Mother's Day. David gives a thumbs-up.

Charlotte and Jett sit silently even though they're sitting side-by-side in the same seats they sat in on the trip out to Phoenix. Jack notices their silence and thinks, *Guess my assumption about a romance fell off the mountain.* He's disappointed.

Charlotte picks up *A Tear and a Smile* by Kahil Gibran, the book she'd brought along to read in case there were any lulls during the traveling. She hadn't opened it until now because most of her days had been spent conversing with Jett.

Jett breaks the silence. "Did you enjoy the meal at Kai's yesterday evening?"

"Yes, Jett, delicious food. And as Jack promised, the view was great," she answers, then returns to reading.

Jett tries to defrost Charlotte's attitude. "I know the call I got during the meal last night upset you even more than you were before. I could have left the table, but I feared that would turn you off even more. I really feel terrible that our friendship has hit a snag. I'd hoped that we could continue to see each other after we get back to Georgia."

She closes the book. "Jett, my feelings are hurt because you weren't honest with me about your work. Dishonesty is not exactly the best way to start a friendship, let alone a meaningful relationship, is it? I thought that you were like me, an artist. Period."

"I agree, Charlotte, but you were so adamant about your penny-pinching that I got the impression that you might be turned off by someone in my position—someone who jets around the world and dines on the finest cuisine—and the opulence of it. Or, on the other hand, you could be a fortune hun—"

"Hunter! You think I might be a penny-pinching fortune hunter? Well, of all the—"

"No, no, I don't! I just wanted to be sure. And I'll tell you right now that I'm sure. You're not!"

"Okay, Jett, but I couldn't help but overhear your phone conversation at Kai's last night, and it sounds like you're in trouble. I heard anger-filled shouts on the other end. Why?"

"Charlotte, I'm vice-president of Deepwell Petroleum. Have been for five years. I worked hard to climb the ladder. And I know I'm fortunate to hold such a position at my age. But I've found that I have no life except work. That's why I chose this tour. I wanted to get away from it all. I really am an artist, a potter mostly, but a painter, too. I know that few artists' lives are luxurious. I don't want to be a bachelor forever. I want a family. My art is the only escape I have from the rat race I'm running. Max and I had a serious argument before I left, and he told me that I'm not indispensable. I may not have a job when I get back. It seems as if I won't."

Charlotte's face reddens. "I heard you adamantly refuse to fly back to Atlanta today. I'm truly sorry. I guess my babble about frugality wasn't very smart, but it's better than being thought of as a fortune hunter."

"Max doesn't even know where I am or what I'm doing, Charlotte! I could be in the North Pole for all he knows. I'm finishing this coach tour because even though you're upset with me, I still want to enjoy your company, if you'll allow me the privilege. Last night was sleepless for me as I considered my options. I made a decision. Fired or not, I'm quitting Deepwell. I'm going to do what I really want to do. I'm sure that you're acquainted with Blue Ridge, aren't you?" Jett questions.

"Sure am, Jett. I've sold some of my artwork at gift shops in

Blue Ridge and Blairsville. And I have several kin who live in Blue Ridge."

"Really? My Aunt Alice and Uncle Zeb live there. Wouldn't it be something if they know each other? Well, it wouldn't be impossible. My uncle is the proprietor of Zeb's Diner. This trip is exactly what I needed, Charlotte. I'm going to check it all out, buy myself a home so I can settle somewhere in the northern Georgia mountains, and open my own pottery studio. I can submit my work and have more shows at Hope Gallery, too. I won't be a starving artist, because I have a worthy financial portfolio and adequate investments."

"Jett, when you gave me your Ziploc bag with the gems you mined, I felt like you didn't care about them at all. I realize now that you do. And if this trip and my contrariness led to you discovering who you really are, then please accept my poutiness as a gift to you. But most of all, please accept my apology for distressing you."

Jett picks up Charlotte's right hand and kisses it. "And will you forgive me for not being upfront about my profession?"

"Yes!" She smiles.

"Thank you, milady."

They both laugh. Jack, who overheard it all, laughs with them.

"You scoundrel, Jack! You were listening, weren't you?" Jett asks.

"Couldn't help it," Jack says. "I think this might be the best part of 'The Amethyst Experience.'"

"I'm really looking forward to the evening dinner cruise on the Mississippi, Jack," Charlotte chimes in. "But we'll almost be home by then, and the trip will be done."

"It's very romantic, young lady," Jack assures her.

Jett feels as if the weight of the world has rolled off his back as he lays his head against the headrest and smiles. He looks over at Charlotte, who is resting her head against the window while she sleeps, her book now on floor. *Well, at least I'm forgiven*, he thinks.

* * *

Albuquerque, San Antonio, and New Orleans are enjoyed by everyone. All of the passengers name the nighttime dinner cruise on the Mississippi the dining highlight of the entire trip.

On the last day, while on their way back to Atlanta, Jett quizzes Charlotte about teaching. "Is it what you expected?"

"I love every moment of it. I've only been at it for four years, but I'm sure I'll always enjoy helping others find their creativity. But honestly, I'd like to do what you plan to do and eventually have my own art studio where I could work with all ages. I'm a solo kid. I think that's why I enjoy teaching. I was born when my parents were in their mid-forties, and they're already gone. Did your father remarry? Do you have brother or sisters?"

Jett grins. "Dad did remarry. Morgan is a good wife for Dad. I have a delightful sister, Becka. She's still unmarried, like me. Charlotte, how is it that you're on this trip when the new schooly-ear has just started?"

"I taught summer art classes for a friend of mine so she could go on her dream trip to Israel. She only teaches in the summer months, so she's filling in for me. But I have to be at work three days after I return. Administration worked it all out for us. I'm curious, Jett, about your given name. I know Jett is short for Jett-son because, as we boarded at the start of this trip, Jack called you Jettson Clarke."

"Mom saw the name in a book of baby names. It means a mineral and/or dark color. I was born with a head full of dark hair, and because she knew that the darkest purple amethyst gems were the most sought-after ones, especially those that have the streaks of red, she decided on that name. She said that Dad immediately announced, 'We'll call him Jett,' so Jett it's been."

"It's uncanny. Your dark hair has some faint streaks of red, too." Charlotte smiles.

He agrees. "It does seem ironic, doesn't it? But I already see wisps of gray, as well."

"Yes, at your sideburns." She grins. "Prematurely grey, as they say."

"I like my name, but I like my middle name, John, better. I appreciate its meaning more. It means gift of God. If I ever have a son, I'd like him to be named John."

"My middle name is Anna. It means favored of God," Charlotte offers.

"I'm wondering..." Jett says. "I know this may sound old-fashioned, but have I been forgiven enough to come courting you? Or at least to have a date or two? Then you can tell me if we can continue. If I have a job, I still plan to spend the next forty-three days of my vacation time chilling out. I know that you need to work, so I can be checking out options for where I can set up shop in the mountains. I will go in to see Max tomorrow so I can tell him my plans and work out my resignation after the forty-three days. Though I expect that my office will be emptied out when I get there. He'll probably tell me that I've lost my mind and that he doesn't want crazies around, anyway. However, I'll tell him that I haven't lost anything. Rather, I've gained much. I'll tell him that if she'll take it, I'm giving my love to a lovely southern belle, one who loves the Lord. What do you think about it, Charlotte?"

"I think that 'The Amethyst Experience' is the nicest thing that's ever happened to me, Jett. We'll just need to let time take its course so we can see if we're indeed those star-crossed artists. The thought of teaching art classes in your mountain potter's studio is sounding mighty good to me. And, Jett, my parents always called me Lottie. If you'd like, you can, too."

Jett smiles and responds eagerly, "I'd like!"

The Fallacious Life of Sadie Pringle

Rebecca Elswick

Sadie Pringle had one ambition—to be an invalid while she was still young and beautiful. Instead of a trunk filled with quilts for her marriage bed, Sadie had filled her hope chest with soft chenille robes, lace-trimmed nightgowns, and several pairs of lounging pajamas that would scandalize her mother if she saw them. She had also collected pairs of movie-star slippers, the kind with the little pompoms on the toes and the tiny heels that would clip-clop when she walked.

Sadie was of the genteel class the future would refer to as "upper-middle," but her small mountain town was not fond of classing off people based on income alone. Money ranked third behind surname and property, so the Pringle family had a stellar pedigree. Like all young ladies of refinement, Sadie was to mind her manners until she was old enough to marry, and then she was to make a good match. After that...well, it was precisely the "after that" Sadie refused to accept.

Since the day Sadie was born, the word peculiar hovered over her head like a cloud of gnats. The only fault her mother deigned claimed as her own was that she was too old when Sadie was born. After having six sons ranging from twenty-eight to fifteen, she closed the book on childbearing, but then, just shy of her fiftieth birthday, Sadie was born. Had it occurred to her, she would have assigned the rightful blame to her husband, but being a simple woman, she took the blame upon herself.

Mrs. Pringle was not from Appalachia, so she thought they lived simply even though the Pringle house was the third largest in town. Mr. Pringle was a lawyer with a small practice that handled civil cases, such as the circumstance of Benjamin Walden's stolen prized rooster. The burden of running the house and raising the children fell upon Mrs. Pringle. With the birth of each son, Mrs. Pringle made the minor adjustments to her daily routine before carrying on as before. Boys were straightforward—feed them and remove potentially harmful obstacles, and they were content, especially when siblings came along as playmates.

This was not the case with Sadie.

Sadie Isabelle Pringle was an elfin child. Her delicate form was a shock to the whole Pringle family, who had been red-cheeked and healthy as children. Her pale flesh glowed as if a network of electrical wires ran under it. Round eyes the color of acorns stared out at the world with marked curiosity. A tiny button nose and a petal-pink mouth completed Sadie's portrait. Her delicate mien was a paradox, for she was a healthy child.

As she grew, she developed a mercurial nature, forming no special attachment to anyone. Her father would walk into a room, see Sadie, and stare like she was an apparition. When Mrs. Pringle rebuked him for not speaking to his daughter, he would say, "But it is Sadie." Her brothers treated her like a puppy, patting her on the head and saying, "There's a nice girl." All but the youngest were married with children of their own, so they found it disconcerting that their children now had a child aunt.

From the beginning, Sadie preferred her own company. She learned to read at age four and began sketching at six, passing her days amid books and sketchpads, her fingers stained with charcoal.

Those who admired the delicate thought the growing Sadie was beautiful. Her hair grew long and lay in layers of auburn curls. Her eyes sparkled with intelligence. In sunlight, her alabaster skin glowed as if sky-blue tincture flowed through her veins. Sadie learned to accent her tenuous appearance, preferring voluminous pastel dresses trimmed with yards of lace and ribbons.

At the age when Sadie should have been learning how to embroider fine linens and set a beautiful table, she was sneaking books out of her father's law office. Sadie scorned her mother's teachings and instead learned how to write an ironclad contract, how to probate a will, and what to do when someone stole your property. When Mrs. Pringle discovered twelve-year-old Sadie reading her father's book about divorce laws, she sent her to Cousin Alberta's cabin in the woods and told her to "make yourself useful."

That proved to be Mrs. Pringle's first mistake.

Cousin Alberta passed her days reading and making lace, her ennui so famous that ten years after she would pass, the family would still speak of her in whispers. Sadie adored her cousin. Her house wasn't a rustic cabin at all, but rather a cottage in a clearing in the woods that was full of flower gardens and apple trees. The cottage was filled with dusty books and curious objects. Cousin Alberta lit candles in the daytime and burned sweet-smelling herbs. Sadie thought this must be what heaven smelled like. Sadie's home smelled of cooked cabbage and tobacco smoke.

There were rumors Alberta had once been jilted at the altar and had gone into seclusion, never reemerging, but all the family knew for sure was that a distant relative had died and left her a tidy sum, enabling her to live independently. Alberta was fiercely private and told the family nothing of her affairs, so they felt inclined to make up their own stories about her miserable life. The collective result was that they decided to feel sorry for Cousin Alberta because she lacked a husband and children, and they left her alone.

Sadie spent every moment she could at Cousin Alberta's, where she discovered the world of novels. Her mother thought too much reading was bad for women. She forbade Sadie to read those "horrible rags," so Sadie spent the winter at Cousin Alberta's reading the classic romantic novels—*Madame Bovary, Pride and Prejudice, Anna Karenina,* and *The Scarlet Letter.* Novels confirmed what Sadie knew in her heart—men would destroy your life. Why else would those beautiful books recount the same tragic story? Each book made it clear that a woman's life was not her own. A girl was first her father's daughter, then her husband's wife, and lastly, a slave to her children.

Sadie had to find a way to escape.

When suitors came calling, Sadie's mother watched in horror as Sadie scorned each one. Mr. and Mrs. Pringle conferred and then sat down with Sadie to have a talk.

Father asked, "Sadie, my dear, why do you refuse these gentlemen's invitations?"

"They are some of the nicest young men in town!" Mother said.

"Idiots! Buffoons!" Sadie said.

"Surely, one of them is...interesting?" Father said. "Malcolm Whitmore—"

Sadie snorted. "Is a horrible, beak-nosed, beady-eyed Bible thumper!"

"Sadie Pringle! How do you know he is horrible? You have not accepted one date!" Mother said. "And then there's that nice Peter Younger. He's—"

"A one-eyebrowed Neanderthal!" Sadie shouted.

"But, child," Father said, "it is time for you to find a husband."

Sadie stood and stamped her foot. "Never." She stared at her parents until the color drained from her mother's face and her father dropped his eyes. Then Sadie wheeled around and strode out of the room.

Mr. Pringle looked at his wife, who burst into tears. She hid her face in her hands and moaned, "Why couldn't she have been a boy? Why?"

Something had to be done.

That night, Mr. and Mrs. Pringle discussed the matter behind their bedroom door. When Mrs. Pringle calmed down, she saw things differently. This was just a silly phase Sadie was going through. Teenage girls were not like teenage boys. At Sadie's age, her brothers had only cared about when the next meal would be served. Teenage girls were full of conflicting emotions. Surely, her daughter wanted what every young woman wanted—a husband and children. This silly notion would pass.

But weeks and then months went by, and Sadie refused every young man's invitation to "step out" until they stopped asking. In a panic, her mother and father sought the advice of Sadie's brothers, who collectively scratched their heads and shrugged, so the brother's wives were consulted.

"Perhaps," said Sadie's eldest sister-in-law, "she spends too much time with her cousin Alberta. So much time with an old woman must be damaging Sadie's spirit."

There was a collective nodding of heads in agreement.

Mrs. Pringle grabbed ahold of this explanation with both hands. "Why, of course," she said, "it's not Sadie's fault. It's that old woman and her scandalous novels that are warping Sadie's senses. We must stop it. It is simple. We'll forbid Sadie to go to Alberta's house."

That proved to be Mrs. Pringle's second mistake.

Sadie wasted no time sneaking out to Cousin Alberta's cottage. She ran straight to Cousin Alberta and threw herself on her feet. Between sobs, she said, "Father and Mother have forbidden me to see you again."

Cousin Alberta nodded and said, "Of course they did."

"There's more. Much more. They want me to get married!"

Again, Cousin Alberta nodded. "Of course they do."

Sadie got down on her knees on the floor and grasped Cousin Alberta's hands. Sadie's pale cheeks were flushed pink, and tears slipped down her face. Alberta thought she had never seen Sadie more beautiful.

"But, Cousin Alberta," Sadie said, "I do not want to get married. I do not want to have children."

"Then, my dear, what do you want to do?"

Sadie leaped to her feet. Her eyes flashed like blue fire. She paced around the room and talked. "On summer mornings, I want to lie in front of the open window and fan myself. When the day's heat becomes unbearable, I want to sit in a cool bath and read a novel. In the evenings, when the fireflies come out of hiding, I want to sketch and sculpt figures from clay. Most of all, I want to study my pleasures, just as my father and brothers studied law, which was their pleasure. Pleasures must mean something. They must be lasting. I do not need the pleasures of the flesh. I do not need riches. I need the freedom to do and be Sadie. Nothing more."

"And what will you do in the winters?" Cousin Alberta asked.

"In the winters, I want to sit in front of the fire and read and sketch. I want to lie under a pile of quilts, with a bag of heated rocks at my feet, and read poetry all night long. I want to read every page of every novel without someone peering over my shoulder. I want to be the Sadie I am meant to be."

Cousin Alberta smiled and motioned for Sadie to come to her. She cupped Sadie's chin in her hand. "Do you think you will eventually tire of that? In a year? Two?"

"Tire? Tire!" Sadie threw her head back and snorted through her nose. "What I would tire of is a husband who expects a hot meal from a smiling wife when he comes home from work. What I would tire of is keeping a house and bearing and raising children." Sadie pounded her chest with her fists. "I have no maternal stirrings in my breast. I want no gold band upon my left hand."

Cousin Alberta drew herself up. Her face transformed into a mask of resolve. She said, "Then leave it to me."

Sadie rejoiced, for she had no doubt that Cousin Alberta was much smarter than her mother and father. Her happiness crashed when Alberta said, "Sadie, you must go home and become a model daughter."

"But I can't," Sadie cried.

Cousin Alberta took Sadie's hands in hers. She said, "It is easier to persuade people to agree with you when they think it's their idea."

"I don't understand."

Cousin Alberta smiled. "You will. Now go home. I will send you messages, and you can leave messages for me. There's a large knot hole in the big scarlet oak tree on the path to my house. Do you know it?"

Sadie nodded. A smile formed on her lips.

Alberta said, "I will send you the plan when I have it all mapped out. Look for my letters in the knot hole. In the meantime, show your parents a new Sadie. You have seen the error of your ways. Be amendable to their instructions, even if it means stepping out with a boy."

"What? No!" Sadie clasped her hands in front of her in prayer position. "Cousin Alberta, please do not make me!"

"Come here, child." Alberta patted the spot next to her on the chaise lounge where she languished under a satin coverlet. "Have I ever done or said anything that harmed you?"

Sadie shook her head.

"Right. Now you are going to go home and begin your transformation. Tell me, were you invited to Anna Peety's birthday party?"

"Yes, but I am not going! I despise her."

Cousin Alberta held up her hand like a stop sign. "That was the old Sadie," she said. "The new Sadie loves parties. You will tell your mother you must have a new dress and talk of nothing else. And then, two days before the party, you will begin to complain of a terrible headache."

As Cousin Alberta explained how Sadie's headache would grow worse on the day of the party—so much worse that Sadie could do nothing but lie in bed with a cool cloth on her forehead—a smile spread across Sadie's face. By the time Cousin Alberta explained that Sadie's headache would become so severe that she would not be able to go to the party, Sadie laughed and clapped her hands.

"One more thing before you go home and become the new Sadie," Cousin Alberta said. "Can you will yourself to cry?"

"I shall go home and practice."

Cousin Alberta smiled. "Of course you will."

Sadie went home and slipped back into her house unnoticed. She ran to her bedroom and opened the closet, gathering up all of her dresses. She spread them across her bed and then went back for her shoes. She opened every dresser drawer and left them open. When her mother came into the room, she was sitting on the floor with her open jewelry box and was crying bitterly.

The transformation had begun.

* * *

Two months later, Sadie was allowed to return to Cousin Alberta's. A message had come to Sadie's mother that said Alberta was ill and asked if she would "please allow my dear cousin Sadie to come and read to me." When Mrs. Pringle told Sadie she could return to Cousin Alberta's, Sadie said, "I will if I have time. I'm very busy with my friends."

Mrs. Pringle smiled. Sadie had finally come to her senses and was acting like a normal girl should.

Sadie sighed a sigh of resignation. "Okay, I will go tomorrow. I can't go today because Walter Moore is coming 'round this evening."

"Of course, dear," Mrs. Pringle said. "You can do whatever you want."

That was Mrs. Pringle's third mistake.

* * *

"You must learn to swoon," Cousin Alberta said. "You are doing well with your headaches, but you must learn how to swoon if you are going to scare off gentlemen callers and convince everyone that you are becoming infirm."

"What must I do?"

"Begin by reading *Dracula*. A lot of swooning is associated with vampires. When you swoon, you must be convincing, and you must be weak and languish afterward. But first, you must begin having spells. Did you gather food and hide it away?"

"I'm ready." Sadie smiled.

* * *

Sadie began to have mysterious spells of weakness. At first, it only happened occasionally, and then she began to have convenient attacks whenever there was a gathering of family and friends. People began to talk. They pointed out her pale skin and slim body. They began to speak of Sadie in whispers. With every headache and every spell of weakness, more rumors about Sadie's declining health circulated.

The doctor was called, and Sadie was told to expect him after lunch. She refused to eat and retired to her room "to rest." For two hours, Sadie exercised. She did jumping jacks and sit-ups, and she ran in place until she was exhausted. She filled a water bottle with scalding water and hid it among the pillows on her bed. When the doctor arrived, he discovered Sadie perspiring in bed, her heart racing. He inquired about how long she had been having these spells, and Sadie confessed it had been happening for quite some time, especially when she got too excited. The doctor patted Sadie on the head and told her she would be just fine, and then he went downstairs and told her parents that Sadie was gravely ill. He prescribed rest and a tonic, saying, "Whatever you do, do not upset the child. I fear this is the beginning of a long illness."

* * *

Sadie's father had stopped saying it was time for her to find a husband and had started looking at her out of the corner of his eye, like he knew a secret about her that was so terrible, he would never reveal it. Sadie hoped that by winter, she could convince her parents to let her move in with Cousin Alberta. She complained constantly about the noise and told her mother she often took a nap at Cousin Alberta's cottage because it was so peaceful there, away from the noise of the town.

Everything was going according to plan until Walter Moore decided he couldn't live without Sadie. It didn't deter Walter in the least that Sadie was too ill to see him. He still rang the bell and inquired about her. He began leaving notes that were written on expensive stationery bearing his family crest. In them, he declared his undying love and promised to wait no matter how long it would take. Horrified, Sadie consulted Cousin Alberta.

"You must tell him you are a hopeless invalid," Cousin Alberta said.

"How is that going to convince him?" Sadie asked.

"It is my experience that people will believe what you tell them to believe," Cousin Alberta said. "It is time to convince everyone that you know you are ill and have accepted your fate."

* * *

With the holiday season approaching, Sadie began refusing food and would take nothing but water and weak tea. In secret, she ate food she had stashed away, so she suffered none, but her parents were frantic. After three days, her mother called the doctor, but Sadie was ready for him. She was lying on the sofa in the parlor, wrapped in a blanket, when he arrived. Just as the doctor was finished examining her, the bell rang, and Sadie knew it was Walter Moore. It was time to swoon.

Walter rushed into the room, thrilled that Sadie had agreed to see him. When he saw the doctor, his face fell. Mrs. Pringle came into the room and tried to hurry the boy and the doctor away.

"It's fine, Mother," Sadie said. She stood, clutching the blanket, and advanced on unsteady feet toward Walter. With all eyes on her, Sadie fell to the floor in a dead faint.

Katherine Hepburn could not have done it better.

When the doctor waved smelling salts under her nose, Sadie's eyes fluttered open, and a low moan escaped her lips. Finally, she managed a weak "What happened?"

"You fainted, dear," said the doctor. "Does something hurt you?"

Sadie slowly raised her arm and pointed to Walter, who was hovering in the background. "He does," she said. "He will not stop coming to my house and writing me letters! He will not leave me alone!" Then she burst into tears.

The doctor grabbed Walter by the arm and marched him from the room. Sadie's mother tried to comfort her daughter, who insisted she must leave at once for Cousin Alberta's. It was the only place where she could rest.

The doctor reappeared. He said, "Sadie, you must have complete quiet so you can rest. I promise you that young man will never bother you again."

Sadie sighed. "Doctor, I want to go to Cousin Alberta's cottage, where it is quiet and peaceful."

The doctor looked at Sadie's mother and said, "Get the child's things ready."

* * *

That evening, Sadie sketched Cousin Alberta as she sat by the fire making lace. A pot of beef stew simmered on the stove, and fresh yeast rolls baked in the oven.

"I have a surprise for you," Cousin Alberta said.

Sadie put down her pencil. "What is it?"

"There are two parcels wrapped in brown paper on my desk. Run and get them."

Sadie left and then danced back into the room carrying two large packages. Together, they tore off the paper to reveal two copies of the latest bestseller, *Gone with the Wind* by Margaret Mitchell.

Sadie squealed and hugged Cousin Alberta, who said, "I thought this would be a good start for our winter reading." She turned to the last page and read aloud, "'After all, tomorrow is another day.'"

Fawn

Courtnee Turner Hoyle

Bobby didn't hear the clacking of hooves or the gentle grunting of birth. She missed the event entirely. She stepped onto her back porch, oblivious to the new life only five feet away. But then something caught her eye as she turned, and she spotted the fawn. She dropped her keys and approached the tiny form. The baby deer could hardly lift its head, and Bobby became concerned. She quietly eased open her door and called the local Wildlife Preservation Office.

She explained her situation to an understanding voice. "I think the baby deer has been abandoned," she said, stroking her own full-term belly.

The wildlife volunteer assured her that the fawn had been left behind intentionally. "The mother should be back for the fawn as evening approaches," she explained. "If not, I can come out and get the baby deer in the morning."

"How early could you be here?" Bobby asked. "I'm supposed to have my labor induced at nine o'clock in the morning."

"Congratulations," the woman told Bobby. "I can pick up the fawn anytime. Just call me."

"This is so strange." Bobby laughed. "I've lived near the Appalachian Mountains my entire life, and I have never had this happen to me."

"You've never found a baby deer on your porch?" The woman chuckled. "It happens more often than you may think. It was hot today, so the mother deer found a cool place to have her fawn. She's probably looking for food right now."

"I have never heard of anything like it," Bobby reiterated.

"You told me you were from Erwin," the woman responded. "I've had a recent call from your area. Last month, a man panicked because he found a baby deer in the back of his pickup truck."

"What happened?"

"I told him to have his wife drive him to work, and the fawn was gone when he came home that evening," the wildlife volunteer said.

"That makes me feel a little better," Bobby admitted. "I was worried that the poor thing had been left behind to fend for itself."

The woman laughed. "No, the mother should be back in a couple of hours. Just try to stay quiet and don't go near the fawn. The mother will be able to smell your scent, and she may be too scared to retrieve her baby."

Bobby wrote down the woman's emergency phone number and promised to call if the baby fawn was still on her porch when she woke up the next morning. The woman advised Bobby not to put out food or water for the deer and wished her luck with her delivery.

Bobby watched the fawn all evening through the large picture window in her den. She eased onto the couch and stared at it as it breathed, lifted its head uneasily, and curled up against the cool bricks that lined her porch. She had been on her way to the store to grab ingredients for her favorite meal when she had noticed the fawn, but she had decided to stay home so she could witness the mother doe's retrieval of her fawn. Plus, she wouldn't disturb the baby deer by leaving and coming back.

Bobby made a peanut butter sandwich and thought about taking it into the living room so she could binge-watch a new mystery series, but she settled on the couch in the den and watched the fawn. She could see the steady movements of its midsection as it breathed easily in its sleep.

"Are you a boy or a girl?" she whispered from her place on the other side of the window.

The fawn lifted its head as if it had heard her voice. Bobby decided that the baby deer was a girl. She couldn't pinpoint her reason for that decision, but maybe it was because she assumed she was carrying a baby girl.

Bobby's mother texted her to confirm the time she would meet her at the hospital. Bobby stared at the message sadly. She had hoped Mark would be able to be with her during labor and delivery, but he had used his leave from the military too early. He was back on assignment in the Navy, and she was stuck with her mother. Bobby loved her mother, but her mother believed she knew more about childbirth than Bobby's obstetrician. Tomorrow was going to be a hard day.

Bobby's stomach tightened, and she braced herself for a Braxton-Hicks contraction. The "practice contraction" was over in under a minute, and the baby moved to signal her distress.

"His *or* her," Bobby corrected herself.

Bobby's mother had been upset when Bobby told her that she and Mark were keeping the baby's sex a secret. Throughout her pregnancy, her mother had continued to mention her desire to know if she was going to have a grandson or a granddaughter.

"You use all this technology every day," she had argued, pointing to Bobby's cell phone, "and you're going to keep my grandchild's gender a mystery."

"Only until birth," Bobby had said, defending herself. "Besides, Mark can't be here for the anatomy ultrasound, so it's only fair to keep the sex of the baby a secret."

Her mother had rolled her eyes, but she had dropped the subject.

Because of his position in the Navy, Mark had more of Bobby's mother's respect than Bobby did as her daughter. Bobby may have been able to avoid many difficult conversations with her mother if she had joined the military like her older brothers had.

The phone rang, startling the baby deer and causing Bobby's baby to jump in her womb. She placed one hand over the phone's speaker and the other hand over her belly.

"Hello, Mom," she whispered.

"Why are you whispering?"

"There's a baby deer on my back porch," Bobby answered.

"That's nice," her mother said, dismissing the miracle. "Did you go to the Outdoor Festival or the Relay for Life?"

"I went to the Outdoor Festival. I bought something for Mark."

"Don't you think you should have stayed home?" her mother said, admonishing her. "There are a lot of people from different places, and you really don't need to expose yourself to so many germs before you give birth. I had my first child during one of the worst flu seasons on record, and I was scared to let anyone near my baby unless I knew they were well."

"It's not cold and flu season, Mother," Bobby countered. "Why did you ask me if I went to the festival if you were going to criticize me for going?"

"I was simply curious," her mother responded haughtily. "What time do I need to be at the hospital?"

"I'm scheduled to arrive at nine," Bobby said.

"I'm excited to meet my grandson soon," her mother said.

"Or grand*daughter*," Bobby emphasized. "I think the baby is a girl."

"Well, you're carrying the baby the same way I carried your brothers," her mother said. "Of course, you would have known for certain if you had asked about the gender during the ultrasound."

"Mom, I'm going to get some rest," Bobby said in an effort to remain even-tempered. "I'll see you in the morning."

"I have one more question," her mother said.

Bobby inhaled deeply and released an inflated sigh. Her mother's "question" could turn into a series of inquiries that she already knew the answers to, or it might lead to an argument.

Her mother took her silence as permission to continue with her query. "Have you thought of a name for the baby?"

Bobby closed her eyes and braced herself for the remark her mother would make after she answered her question. Bobby and Mark had tossed around possible baby names for each sex, but none of the names seemed to fit.

"I'm going to see the baby before I decide on a name," Bobby replied.

"Choosing names for the baby would be easier it you knew the gender of the child," her mother shot back. "I had names picked out and sewn onto blankets before you and your brothers were born."

"That was considerate of you," Bobby said, hoping to avoid an argument. "I'm going to eat before it gets too late." It seemed like a necessary lie.

Bobby thought the mention of food would keep her mother from extending the conversation, and she was right. Her mother allowed their talk to end pleasantly after warning Bobby of the hazards of eating too close to labor, then contradicting her assertion by telling Bobby that she needed to have snacks to maintain her energy.

Bobby spent the golden hours of the evening watching the baby deer's steady breaths. She thought about Mark, and she wondered if he would be able to contact her. He had received a two-week leave, but the consent had been given a little too early. Mark had arrived home when Bobby was thirty-eight weeks pregnant. Bobby's pregnancy had been considered full-term by her doctors, and her mother had urged her to have her labor induced while Mark was home from the military, but Bobby had wanted her labor to begin naturally.

"Mothers with husbands in the military schedule inductions all the time," her mother had said, urging her. "Don't you want Mark to see the birth of his son?"

"I want the baby to pick *his or her* own birthday," Bobby had countered.

Now, in the dimming light on the last full day of her pregnancy, Bobby doubted her decision. She wanted Mark's warm hand around her own, and she wanted his voice to coach her through each wave of pain.

The sounds from the Relay for Life echoed off the mountains that surrounded her neighborhood. A local bluegrass band played a beat that was almost familiar. Bobby considered walking the short distance to the local track and joining the walk. After all, her father had recently passed away from lung cancer. She could walk a lap in his memory and strengthen her muscles for labor and delivery.

But Bobby decided there were too many people at the track. Several people might recognize her, and they might try to talk to her about Mark and their baby. She had no desire to have redundant conversations with different people. She didn't want to hear people say, "Haven't you had the baby yet?" Bobby was eight days past her due date, and she grew tired of explaining that a normal gestation lasted between thirty-eight and forty-two weeks. It had been hard enough to explain the delay to her mother every morning when she called Bobby for an update on her pregnancy.

"I had all of my children *before* I was forty weeks pregnant," Bobby's mother informed her every day. "I guess my body just knew what it was doing."

Another Braxton-Hicks contraction tensed her stomach. It was more intense than her previous practice contractions, but it was gone in less than thirty seconds.

Bobby thought about lying to her mother and telling her that the induction had been postponed for another day, but she couldn't do it. It was better to have her mother constantly berate her than to be alone.

Another practice contraction tightened her stomach, and Bobby lost her breath. She waited until it ended and then opened a bottle of water. She drank half of the bottle at once and lay down on her left side. She counted out five minutes without a contraction. She watched the shadows of the leaves on the trees dance across the wooden floorboards of her den. She imagined dancing with them in perfect harmony out in the encouraging wind.

A rustle from just outside the window grabbed her attention, and she rose to look. From her vantage point, she could see the baby deer. It raised its head and seemed to sniff the air. Beside the fawn was a small pot that contained the remnants of a failed attempt to transplant one of her mother's citronella plants, and the fawn craned its neck to chew at the tough, dry leftovers. Finding no sustenance, the deer seemed to fold its feet beneath itself, and then it abruptly rose. Bobby watched in wonder as the fawn stood on wobbly legs and glanced around the porch. The miracle was short-lived. The baby shakily returned to its previous position.

Bobby hardly felt her stomach tighten again as she watched the deer drift to sleep, but the end of the contraction was uncomfortable, and it brought her back to her position on the couch. Her doctor had explained to her that she should drink water and either lie on her left side or walk around if she experienced a lot of Braxton-Hicks contractions, so Bobby rose and walked the length of her house. The bluegrass music was clearer on the other end of her house. A plastic bear full of honey seemed to mock the contraction that stopped her.

Bobby had visited the town's Outdoor Festival earlier that day, in search of local honey. She had purchased a medium-sized bottle of honey from a nice couple who lived only two miles away. Bobby had walked in the blazing sun much longer than she had intended, and she had carried a heavy bag of candles and crafts through most of the downtown area.

I'm in labor, she realized.

Bobby's mind flew into a flurry of thoughts. She hadn't finished packing her hospital bag, she needed to call her mother, and she had to alert the hospital.

Bobby grabbed the counter as another contraction blocked logical thoughts. It eased after a minute. The contractions were coming quickly, and they were less than five minutes apart. Bobby used the time between contractions to ease her way to the couch in the den. She reached for her phone and felt a surge of warm fluid soak her shorts. She removed her shorts and shuffled her way to the bathroom for a towel. She carried her phone in one hand and her soaked shorts and underwear in the other.

Bobby caught a glimpse of herself in the mirror and decided to take one more picture of her pregnancy belly before her baby was delivered. She waited through another contraction that seemed to pull her hips at both ends. It left a lasting ache in her pelvis. She snapped a picture of herself in the mirror and wondered how her mother had managed labor pains four different times. She carried a towel and her phone to the couch. She was able to fold the towel and sit on it before another wave of birth pain enveloped her.

The baby deer had awakened and was sitting with its head erect. Its posture was stiff, and its ear twitched as gnats tried to invade it.

Through her pain, Bobby stared at the phone and wondered who to call. Erwin had almost transitioned from using another county's ambulance service to using their own service, but it didn't matter, as Bobby's contractions were too frequent. An ambulance wouldn't reach her on time. Her mother lived five miles away, but she would not leave until she called Bobby's brothers to let them know about her labor. Besides, what if the smell of all the first responders or her mother's strong perfume kept the fawn's mother away?

Bobby changed positions on the couch so she could monitor the fawn. It was easier to handle her contractions when she was distracted by the baby deer's movements. It took almost all of her energy to pull herself through each contraction.

She wanted to go to the hospital. She wanted to be assured that the pain she was feeling was normal and that her labor was progressing naturally, but she couldn't bring herself to move from her chosen position or pick up her phone. The contractions were too intense to talk through, and she needed every breath between contractions to prepare for the next one.

Bobby thought she saw the shadow of another form at the edge of her porch. She tried to focus on it, but her body was distracted by the constant pain she felt.

Suddenly, Bobby felt her baby's head drop. Her mother had told her that she had "dropped," but she had been referring to the profile of Bobby's belly. Bobby was experiencing the baby's head dropping into the birth canal. She understood now that going to the hospital was no longer an option. Her baby would be born soon.

Bobby had read about the common medical emergencies that could happen during a birth. The baby could need assistance exiting the birth canal, or it could need medical attention or general care that Bobby was unfamiliar with. Bobby could tear at the delivery site or hemorrhage during or after the birth. She was terrified about her situation, but she was at the mercy of each powerful contraction. She finally succumbed to their assertive nudges.

Bobby wanted to move onto the floor, but her body would not allow it. Every contraction seemed to edge the baby's head closer to emergence. She felt an urge to push, but fear kept her fighting against the contractions. She wanted to deliver her baby, but she was scared to do it by herself.

Bobby wasn't alone, though. The shadow moved, and a doe stepped within view of the window. She cocked her head to the side, and her ears twitched as if she could hear the sounds of accouchement inside the house. Earlier that day, the doe had given birth to the fawn on Bobby's back porch. She had delivered the baby deer without fanfare or help. Bobby decided she would push one time to honor the doe's natural achievement. It was a mostly irrational thought, but

Bobby's suffering was too great to keep her from dismissing the idea.

Bobby pulled herself into a squatting position on the couch. It took a lot of energy to fight against the residual tenderness from her most recent contraction, steady one arm on the back of the couch, and grab the armrest with her other hand. She felt discomfort in her midsection. She locked eyes with the mother deer and pushed. She could feel her baby leave her body in a rush. She tilted to catch the baby and pulled the baby to her. Bobby had no idea how long she rocked the screaming infant while she repeated, "We did it." She wrapped the baby in the towel and offered her breast to her newborn.

Bobby looked out the window at the expected twilight. The baby deer was on its feet again, but this time it took wobbly steps toward its mother. Bobby watched its first steps as she held her baby to her breast. The doe waited patiently for her progeny and dipped her head when the fawn managed the only step off of Bobby's back porch. The mother deer seemed to look back at Bobby. The wise doe stared in her direction for only a moment before she guided her fawn to the safety of the woods.

Bobby gazed into the face of her infant. The tiny eyes stayed closed, but the eyebrows furrowed, and the little body rested peacefully against her chest. She moved one of the legs and exposed the answer to the question everyone had been asking.

Bobby gave into her feelings and allowed the tears to slide down her face. Her circumstances had caused a roller coaster of emotions, and she took a moment to be overjoyed by her new baby and proud of herself for delivering her baby without assistance. She had experienced two miracles in one day. A mother deer had given birth on her back porch, and Bobby had given birth in her home. Was there a greater feeling? There had been so much pain, but the efforts of labor were forgotten in the bliss of birth.

The baby sighed in easy slumber. Bobby looked out into the woods and held her infant, thankful for her daughter, Fawn.

FHB

Lynda A. Holmes

Ida Fay looked up and wiped her brow, giving her fingers a break from shucking fresh ears of corn. It was summer, and the mountain air was dewy clean after a morning rain. Although Ida was glad school was out for the season, she missed seeing her friends.

Her gaze spanned across the road that started at the log house and went down Lookout Mountain. What looked like a speck on the dirt road gradually became a horse-drawn wagon carrying two grown-ups and some children. Ida Fay set down her bowl and blinked her eyes twice. The wagon was still there. Finally, she recognized Preacher Wayne, his wife, and their three children, and she saw a baby's arm sticking out. She waved at them, and they waved back, the older children shouting, "Hey, Ida!" Ida was thrilled to get to see Julie, the eldest of the preacher's children. Julie was the closest in age to Ida, who was thirteen. The preacher had announced at the monthly service last week that the baby was old enough for them to begin visiting again. Who knew it would be so soon?

"Mama, we've got company. It's Preacher Wayne and the whole family," Ida shouted through the doorway of the log cabin.

Mama appeared, along with Ida's younger brother, Joel, who was hanging on to her skirt. "Good Lord in heaven. When the preacher said they were ready to begin visiting again, he wasn't joking."

Mama pushed Joel over to Ida and dashed out to meet the family, patting her hair back into place. Ida shushed Joel and gave him an ear of corn so he could investigate.

The visitors most likely planned to stay for supper. Mama would need her help, and Julie would help, too. They might even have some fun. Supper would certainly require FHB this evening. She would remind Papa and Brax, her oldest brother, while everyone washed up for supper. Papa and Brax would be out mending fences for several more hours. As long as Ida, Mama, Papa, and Brax followed FHB, there would be enough corn soup, greens, and drop bread to feed everyone. Mama did a good job of making their limited bounty go around. Sometimes a whole meal was cornbread, buttermilk, and collard greens. Friends and family were welcome no matter what.

The wagon pulled up beside the porch of the log house, and the preacher pulled the horse to a halt. Dust flew and settled while Mama took the baby and the preacher helped Mrs. Wayne down from the passenger seat. Their six-year-old boy, Terence, ran after the clucking chickens that had been minding their own business in the side yard. Joel ran after Terence and the chickens. Ida hugged Julie, and they started catching up on all of the happenings in both families this summer.

"Well, what a nice surprise for you all to visit us," Mama declared as she hugged Mrs. Wayne. "The men are out fence mending today. They will join us for supper. Just tell me the news from town since last Sunday's service."

Mama handed the babe to Ida Fay and Julie. Preacher Wayne turned to lead their horse to the water barrel and then walked out through the field to find Papa and Brax.

"What's the baby's name?" Ida asked.

"This is Pauline," Mrs. Wayne said as she tweaked the baby's cheek. "She just finished nursing, so it's about naptime."

Ida Fay gave Mama the bowl of corn and nodded at her. While Jesus set an example by multiplying a few loaves and fishes for the multitudes, Ida's family used FHB. Mama had learned it from her own mama while growing up on a farm in rural Georgia where they grew their own food and raised chickens, hogs, and cows.

Mama could do almost anything. Ida remembered one time when a needle had broken off in Mama's hand while she was sewing lace decorations on boxes so that Ida and Brax could participate in the boxed lunch fundraising dinner at school. The prettiest boxes always brought in more money even though every box included tasty country cooking, including fried chicken or bacon and lard biscuits or cornbread. Mama hadn't cried, but she had looked pale and had lain down for a spell while Papa got in the wagon with the children and the boxed lunches and took them on over to the school for the festivities. Papa had driven Mama to the nearest doctor while their teacher, Miss Telly, looked after the school crowd. Mama had waved slightly with her good hand, keeping the wounded hand motionless in her lap. Ida Fay had cried but waved back, wiping the tears off her face. She had to carry on, just like Mama.

The box lunch that had caused Mama's accident with the needle had brought in several dollars that day, and that had helped pay for the doctor visit. People had chipped in out of respect for Mama. The community helped look after its own.

Ida Fay sighed, remembering how Mama's hand had been bandaged for a long time after that event. It must have been painful, but she had never complained. Finally, the wound had healed, leaving nothing but a tiny scar and the memory.

Ida's thoughts shifted back to the present as Julie shifted a sleeping Pauline to her shoulder without waking her. Ida led Julie inside the cabin and took her to her own bed, where Pauline could nap in the quiet. Julie tenderly laid the baby girl down, touching her softly and whispering, "That's a good girl."

"We better get back outside so we can try to keep up with Joel and Terence," Ida said to Julie.

The girls played tag with the young boys, followed by hide-and-seek. Terence showed Joel his marbles and taught him how to play with them. One of them was a cat's eye marble. Joel showed Terence his big hoop and taught him how to roll it back and forth through the yard. The boys got along together just fine.

"Ida Fay, I need you and Julie to see if you can ring the neck of one of those hens for supper," Mama said, and then she disappeared into the house when she and Mrs. Wayne heard Pauline wake up and cry a bit.

The girls looked at one another and answered, "Yes, ma'am."

Ida Fey wondered if they could follow through with the task. Neither girl had ever rung a chicken's neck, so they had no idea what would happen.

Julie watched as Ida began chasing the hens, figuring out how to catch one of them before they scattered away. Try as she might, Ida could not hold on to the hen long enough to do anything with it. Neither could Julie. The hens flew up and scattered every time the girls moved closer to them. They seemed to know that the future might not be very rosy for them.

Ida Fey could see that Mama was now holding a wide-awake Pauline and singing to her inside the house. Mrs. Wayne watched from her chair beside the doorway, smiling and chatting with Mama. Suddenly, Mrs. Wayne rolled up her sleeves and marched out to the side yard, shooing Ida and Julie back toward the house. In a flash, Mrs. Wayne caught one of the hens, rang its neck, and proceeded into the house with it.

Mrs. Wayne and Mama talked and laughed as they plucked the chicken piece-by-piece over a hearth fire, preparing to fry it. The girls played with Pauline and kept an eye on Joel and Terence.

That evening, Ida Fay sidled up beside Papa and Brax as they washed up for supper. "FHB with the corn soup and greens and bread fixins," she whispered, waiting for them to nod their understanding.

Papa winked at Ida as he nodded back at her.

Ida giggled, loving the way Papa made her feel like everything would be all right.

Julie stared at Ida. "What were you whispering to your pa and Brax?" she asked.

Ida Fay said, "Shhh. It has to be a secret until after supper. Then I'll tell you, but only if you swear to keep it between us. It's real important." Then she said in a loud voice, "Plenty of fried chicken tonight, thanks to Mrs. Wayne and Mama. They've been working on that bird all afternoon."

After everyone was cleaned up and ready, they gathered around the table. Preacher Wayne gave thanks for their blessings. Mama passed around the plates and fried chicken pieces, then the bowls full of corn soup, greens, and bread. The evening meal was a success, thanks to FHB. Papa played a tune on his juice harp, and they sang a couple of their favorite hymns together.

When the dishes were washed and put away and the Wayne family was loading up the wagon to ride home, Ida Fay hugged Julie one last time.

Julie whispered to Ida, "Okay, you can tell me the secret. I promise I'll keep it. Cross my heart."

Just before Preacher Wayne snapped the horse's reins, Ida Fay whispered to Julie, "When we have unexpected company, we always have enough food as long as we practice FHB: Family Holdback."

Help Me

Linda Hudson Hoagland

There is nothing more uncomfortable than driving down a deserted stretch of highway with a full bladder. Guys have it easy. They can pull over anywhere, discreetly pull it out, and go. Women have to make a production of untying, zipping, pulling, and who knows what else. Not to mention, we have to worry about some freak jumping out of the bushes. But I couldn't hold it anymore. In hindsight, I should have just peed my pants and kept going, but how could I have known?

* * *

It was dark, and I was in pain because of my overloaded bladder. That last cup of iced tea had done it. "Please, please let there be a rest stop or a convenience store up ahead," I prayed. *No such luck. God must be mad at me for not going to church,* I thought as I wriggled around in my seat. "I have to do something. It has to be now, or it will be too late," I mumbled.

I guided my car onto the berm, where I jumped out of the driver's seat and ran to the passenger side of the car. I stepped down into a drainage ditch where I thought I might have a little more privacy. My foot brushed against something that was not green and leafy. I tried to suppress the scream that was trying to surface from my soul. *Oh God, what is that?* I thought as I jerked my foot away from whatever it was. Then I felt it grab my ankle. This time, I did scream as loud as my throat and lungs would allow. It released my ankle, and I tried to scramble out of the ditch.

"Help me," whispered a weak voice.

I stopped mid-step and turned around to see the source of the whisper. Of course, I couldn't see anything because it was so dark. Not even the light of the moon or stars existed in the overcast sky.

"I'll be right back. I need to get a flashlight," I said as I climbed out of the ditch.

I headed back to my car and paused as I reached for the handle to open the car door. *Should I just get in and move on*, I asked myself. Of course I wasn't going to leave. I had to find out who was in that ditch. I grabbed my flashlight from the glove box and headed back to the ditch. All thoughts of a full bladder had left my mind. When I returned to the ditch, I shined the light toward the area where I had been. I saw her there. At least, I thought it was a her. She was covered with dirt and blood. I walked slowly toward her, taking in what I could with my eyes. I was amazed that she was still alive after receiving all of the cuts and abrasions that were on her body.

"Can you move?" I whispered as I kneeled next to her.

"No," she replied in a barely audible whisper.

While I had been retrieving my flashlight, I had also grabbed my cell phone. I dialed 9-1-1.

"What is your emergency?" asked the gruff voice of a man.

"I'm on Route one-thirty-nine, and I found an injured person lying in a ditch," I said quickly.

"Where on Route one-thirty-nine?" he asked.

"I really don't know anything except that I'm nowhere near a town," I answered.

"What is your name?" asked the operator.

"Maggie Stevens. Please hurry," I begged.

"Maggie, look around and see if you can spot any type of land-mark," instructed the 9-1-1 operator.

"It's dark out here, mister. No cars have even driven by since I pulled over onto the berm," I said with exasperation.

"You are probably on the straight stretch of road between Still-well and Dry Fork. I'll send the ambulance out. The deputies are already on their way," said the operator.

"Please hurry. I don't think she will make it without help. A lot of help," I said sadly and softly. I hung up and turned to the young lady in the ditch. "What is your name?" I was trying to keep her talk-ing so she would remain conscious.

She moaned and tried to speak.

"Stay with me," I whispered calmly.

She moaned again and said, "Mary."

"Mary, what is your last name? I need it so I can tell the ambu-lance people."

"Johnson," she said with a painful sigh.

"Mary, what happened?"

"Jack tried to kill me," she said weakly.

"Do you have anyone I can call?" I asked as I watched her fading away.

"Mother. Emma Saranden," she said.

"Do you have any children?" I asked.

"Yes, with mother," she said as she shut down.

I knew I would not be able to talk to her again.

I saw the blue flashing lights of the police car, and I waved them down so they would know to come to a stop behind my car. I pointed to Mary Johnson and told them everything she had told me. When they saw her, they checked on the ambulance's estimated time of arrival and told them that it was an extreme emergency. When I told them that I'd found her only because I had stopped to find a place to empty my bladder, they had a good chuckle. They took my personal information so they could contact me at a later date.

"I want to stay until the ambulance gets here," I mumbled. "I told her I wouldn't leave."

Finally, the ambulance came to the spot, and the EMTs took one look at her and loaded her into the back. I felt sure they didn't think she would make it to the hospital. When they had her loaded and were getting ready to transport her, I finally climbed into my car. I drove for a couple of miles and located a convenience store. Inside, I headed directly into the ladies' room.

After returning to my car, I drove a few more miles and arrived at my destination: home. After feeding my cats and closing the blinds, I grabbed my phone so I could call Stillwell Community Hospital.

"I'm checking on Mary Johnson. She should be in the emergency room. I'm the person who found her in a ditch along the side of the road," I said in a flurry of words.

"Are you a family member?" asked the professional-sounding person who answered the call.

"No, I tried to help her. I want to make sure she is all right," I explained.

"I'm sorry, but I can't release any information about her condition over the telephone, especially if you are not a family member," explained the hospital employee.

"Tell me this, is she in the emergency room?" I asked, frustration flooding through me.

"I'm sorry, ma'am. I can't tell you that."

At that point, I hung up the telephone. I walked back outside to my car and made the short drive to the hospital. I walked through the emergency room door and was stopped by an attentive nurse.

"You can't come in here," she said sternly.

"I'm looking for my sister, Mary Johnson. Is she here?" I asked, lying so I could find out how Mary was doing.

"She is behind that curtain, but you can't see her now. The doctors are working with her. You will need to go to the waiting room.

We will come out to talk with family members when we can," the nurse said as she turned to go inside the curtained area.

I went to the waiting room. No one else was there, meaning that no family members had showed up to check on Mary. I wondered if they even knew she was in the emergency room. I couldn't go home without knowing Mary's condition, so I found an almost-comfortable chair, sat, and waited. The doctor did not come in to speak with me, but the deputy showed up in all of his glory.

"Are you Maggie Stevens?" he asked sternly as he maintained eye contact.

"Yes, sir," I answered, staring back at him to let him know that I didn't feel intimidated by his demeanor.

"Tell me how you discovered the victim," he said as he cast his eyes to the floor to break the intense stare.

"Well, like I told the other deputy, I found her lying in the ditch," I said reluctantly. I knew he would want to know why I stopped there.

"Why did you pull over, ma'am?" he asked as he held up his notepad, his pen poised to write.

"I had to relieve myself," I said in a mumble.

"You what?" he asked as a smile started to curl his lips.

"I had to go pee," I said loudly. "I didn't think I could wait any longer."

"That was a fortunate call of nature for the victim. Had you ever met her, the victim, before you discovered her in that ditch?"

"No, sir."

"Mary Johnson, the young lady, is asking to see you. Do you feel like talking with her?" he asked solemnly.

"Yes, sir."

I followed the deputy to a room in ICU. I watched the nurse cover Mary's face with a blanket and step away from the bed. The deputy stepped up to the bed and pulled the blanket from Mary's devastated face. That was when I realized she was dead. Tears erupted from my soul because I had wanted Mary to live and testify against Jack so he would receive the punishment he deserved.

"Ms. Stevens, you will be called upon to testify so that the man who did this can be prosecuted. Can you help us?" the deputy asked.

"I certainly can. I will do it for Mary."

Marathon of Hope

Courtnee Turner Hoyle

R ose stretched her arms and airways. The snow-tipped mountains contradicted the change of the season in the valley. She breathed in the subtle springtime humidity and prepared for a sweaty afternoon run. She had jogged laps on the same route every day for months. She started at her home, which was just outside of town, one block from where the town's annual Apple Festival drew thousands of visitors every fall. Last year had been the first year she could remember that she hadn't gone to the festival. It had been a difficult time in her life.

* * *

After several months at home, with only occasional Skype calls and phone calls with her son, she received a message from her doctor. The doctor asked Rose to visit her office the following week. Rose kept all of her yearly appointments, so she wondered about the need for the consultation. After almost a week of anxious anticipation, Rose wrung her hands in the doctor's office. The doctor told

Rose that a lump had been detected during her last mammogram, but they had caught it early. Rose did not remember anything else about the conversation. Her ears rang through the doctor's words, and she only thought of all of the possible outcomes.

Two months, one surgery, and a scan later, the worst was confirmed. Her doctor gave her a timeline and a schedule. Rose had options for a longer life, but she shouldn't make long-range plans.

Her son, Andrew, requested a leave from the Navy so he could marry his high school girlfriend, Beth. Rose understood that her sickness was speeding up their plans for matrimony, but it didn't lessen their commitment. Andrew's decision didn't surprise Rose. He always won her favor through his actions, and the community embraced him.

Rose had been a single mother, and the neighbors had helped her keep an extra eye on Andrew. Once, after she had sent him to his room as punishment for pulling the cat's tail, the couple across the street had sent her a picture of Andrew standing in his window naked. She had wondered if that was the reason that they had remained childless.

Over the years, Rose and Andrew had learned about plants together in the neighborhood garden. Rose was always watering tomato plants with a hose, and Andrew was finding more colorful ways to water the plants and winning first prize for the largest pumpkin at the Apple Festival. Rose and Andrew had grown together through their efforts. There had been many bumps along the way. She and Andrew had planted sunchokes, and they had taken over their first garden. Rose had not realized that sunchokes were invasive, and she had been angry at herself for the mistake.

Andrew had patted her back one morning as she had stared out at her blunder, and she had cried, "I don't know how I will fix this."

"You will make it happen, Mommy," he had said, consoling her before bouncing off with his toy boat.

Another time, Andrew had ripped up an arugula plant from the ground. He had carried it into the house triumphantly. Rose had gasped, but she hadn't let him know that he was supposed to pick the leaves. The only salad they had shared from that plant was delicious.

The year he had graduated, Rose had purchased four zucchini plants. She and Andrew had harvested more zucchinis than they could eat in that year. Andrew had suggested giving them to the neighbors, and the community had dubbed them "The Zucchini Family."

Andrew was always full of kindness. He had mowed lawns to raise money for a bicycle, and then he had used the bicycle to deliver food and supplies to people who could not leave their homes. As a high school freshman, he had suggested planting food-bearing trees in the downtown area with his high school agriculture group. The trees they had planted gave fruit to the displaced people in the community every year.

Rose had been convinced that no one would be good enough for her son, but she had changed her mind quickly when Andrew had brought Beth home to meet her. Beth had been just as considerate and caring as Andrew, and Rose had been happy to watch their romance blossom and grow.

Andrew had joined the Navy as soon as he graduated high school. Rose and Beth missed him terribly, but they supported his dream. They leaned on each other when Andrew was at sea, and they shared Skype calls and teary-eyed phone calls with him.

When Andrew was on leave, he was devoted to the women in his life, continuing to help Rose in the garden and yodeling love songs to Beth from the shower. When he was at sea, Andrew would send Rose and Beth handwritten letters, and they would share them with each other.

After her diagnosis, Andrew and Beth skipped their honeymoon to spend more time with Rose. Rose begged them to go to a tropical island, but Andrew insisted that they would rather be with her.

When it was time for Andrew to return to his post, Rose did not want to let go of him. "What if I don't see you again?" she said.

Andrew smiled at his mother. "You'll make it happen," he assured her. He left confidently, never doubting his words.

In Andrew's absence, Beth visited Rose frequently. They cooked dinner together at least three times a week. Beth had read that cancer patients could benefit from reducing the amount of sugar in their diets, so Rose eliminated almost all of the unnatural sugars from her foods. Rose took Beth hiking on her favorite trails, and Beth encouraged her to join a cancer support group.

Rose's support group met virtually every week, and she looked forward to their conversations. She especially liked the coordinator of the group, Bridget, and they spent many afternoons talking over the phone. Bridget suggested that she enter the Marathon of Hope event after Rose spoke to her about the hikes she had shared with Beth. It would be held in the spring, so she would have plenty of time to train.

"My doctor counseled me not to make long-range plans," Rose informed her.

Bridget paused, searching for the best words. "Why don't you train for the event, and if you show up that day, I'll let you run."

Rose settled for the compromise. Besides, she doubted she would win if she tried to press her point further.

Rose started training for the marathon just before Thanksgiving. Andrew was stationed on his ship during the holiday, but he promised to be home for Christmas. A week later, Beth met him at a port to celebrate the holiday and buy Christmas presents. Rose had told him about the marathon during a call.

"I'll have to go running with you," he teased when he saw her. "We'll see if you can outrun a Navy man."

* * *

Rose stumbled as she reflected on the memory, and she blamed it on a break in the sidewalk. She waved at a man on a porch. He had witnessed her misstep.

"When's the race?" he called.

"Tomorrow morning!" she yelled back.

Rose quickened her pace. Dogwoods seemed to smile at her as she breezed past them. She turned the corner and rested in her driveway, her hands on her knees. After a series of cooldown exercises, she entered her house and went through her nightly routine.

This race meant more to her than she wanted to admit. It was something that she had hoped she would be alive to do, but more importantly, she had promised Andrew that she would run in the marathon.

* * *

A week after Thanksgiving, Rose visited her doctor for an appointment so they could discuss the progression of the cancer. She had almost canceled the appointment. She didn't want to have more bad news staring at her while she tried to enjoy the Christmas season.

Her doctor sat down, a complicated look on her face. "Your tests show that you are in remission," she revealed. "Congratulations."

Rose erupted with questions. In the end, it was surmised that the disease had not been detected in her last scan.

"I thought there was no real hope of a future," Rose said.

"Sometimes this happens," the doctor explained. "Treatments that are meant to prolong a person's life can end up providing a miracle."

The doctor probably expected Rose to be elated, but she left the office more confused than relieved. Were the results real? Would the disease come back?

Andrew was excited when she told him over Skype later. Beth

was with her, and tears and hugs flowed freely.

"This means we can all go to Hawaii on our honeymoon!" Andrew announced.

"Wait," Rose argued. "A honeymoon is for the newlyweds to spend time together."

"We'll have plenty of time together," Andrew said. "You can practice for your marathon by running on the beach, and Beth and I can sip fruity drinks and dance the night away." He mimicked dancing with his wife on the screen, and Beth and Rose giggled at his mirth.

* * *

Rose lay down on her bed, and a tear slid from her eye, landing on her pillow. She closed her eyes against the pain, but it overwhelmed her.

* * *

Rose had not been expecting Beth's call. She didn't remember what she had done when Beth collapsed on her porch in tears. Andrew's funeral was two days before Christmas, the day he had been scheduled to come home. Rose sat by the flag-covered coffin with an empty heart. Her son had been her whole life, and he had only been twenty-two years old. How could a simple fall have extinguished his light?

She was mad at the Navy. She was mad at the crew members who had been on the ship with her son when an accident had taken his life. She was mad at Beth because she was the last family member to see him alive. She was mad at herself.

Why couldn't it have been me? she asked God in her prayers every night. Why should I get to live when he had so much left to do?

After the funeral, Rose pulled away from her life. She stayed home, wrapped in a blanket, and slept. She stopped attending the virtual cancer meetings. She couldn't accept condolences from her newfound friends. The only thing that gave her solace was pretending that Andrew was still at sea, and that meant that she couldn't face anyone who had known him. Beth had tried to comfort Rose after the funeral, but Rose had avoided her. Beth would be a constant reminder that Andrew would never come home.

After a month passed, Bridget contacted her. She wanted to provide Rose with the map for the run.

"I don't think I'm going to do it anymore," Rose told her. "My cancer is gone, and Andrew's..."

"You are still a cancer survivor," she reminded Rose. "You have a place in the race if you want to be there." Bridget swallowed hard. "We all loved Andrew. I think he would have been proud to have seen you run in the race."

Rose thought a long time about her conversation with Bridget. She started training for the marathon the following week, careful to avoid any paths that reminded her of Andrew. Beth continued to call her, but Rose erased the messages without listening to them. It was easier to lose her kinship with Beth than it would be to immerse herself in her son's death again. Every run left her alone in her thoughts, though. And her mind always went back to her son.

She could almost hear him sometimes. "Speed up," Andrew would tell her in her mind. "You have to beat this Navy boy."

Rose told herself that every lap held new possibilities, and she longed to apply it to her life, but her grief kept her running in the same circles. Most of her runs ended with her in a sweaty mess, having overexerted herself while she tried to get away from the pain. Her neighbors lifted her off the sidewalk more than once to guide her into her house.

One of the benefits of the hard runs was that she could fall asleep easily. She would lie down and dream of Andrew. It was the only comfort she had left.

One day after work, Beth was waiting for Rose on her porch. "Please don't shut me out," she begged. "I need you. Andrew's gone, and I want to talk to someone who remembers him."

Rose brushed past her and shut the door behind her. She listened to Beth sob on the other side of the door, not comforting her, but unwilling to move away. Finally, Beth went home.

* * *

It was harder for Rose to fall asleep on the night before the race. She tossed and turned until the twilight in her mind finally darkened to night. She dreamed of Andrew. He appeared on what she imagined was his Navy ship. He leaned over the railing, staring at the sea. The dark waves bounced off the ship while the wind whipped his glossy black hair. Rose shielded her eyes from the sunlight around her son.

"Hey, Mom," he said simply, turning to face her.

Rose almost tackled him. His embrace felt warm and real. "I want to trade places with you," she begged him. "I was the one who was supposed to die, not you."

"You are exactly where you are supposed to be," he insisted. "I had my time, and I would have liked to have stayed longer, but I'm happy with my legacy."

"But I love you," Rose choked out. "I wanted you to have children and grow old with Beth."

Andrew smiled sadly. "Everyone doesn't get to live a *long* life, but they can still have a *full* life," he replied. "I was able to see all of this." His gaze shifted, and his hand swept out to indicate the sea and everything that lay beyond it. "And I got to come home to you and Beth."

"But there's so much you could have done," Rose argued.

"Maybe," Andrew agreed. "But I'm happy with the time I had."

Rose struggled with the feelings she wanted to express to her son. Nothing compared to the words he had spoken. "But I love you," she said lamely.

Andrew humored his mother with a smile. "I love you, too, but now you can share your love for me with Beth."

Rose looked away sharply after the mention of her daughter-in-law.

"What is it?" he asked.

"I haven't spoken to Beth," she answered truthfully.

Andrew moved away from her and ran a hand through his hair. He cut his eyes in her direction and shook his head. He settled on a bench, his head in his hands. "Do you know what kept me going when I was on the ship for months at a time?" he asked.

Rose shook her head. She was already beginning to feel Andrew's disappointment.

"I knew that you and Beth were together," he confided. "You would tell me about all of your dinners and hikes with her, and she would tell me how much she loved borrowing my mom."

Unexpected tears slid from Rose's eyes. She hadn't known that Beth thought of her that way. "It's just so hard to be around her without thinking of you," she defended.

Andrew looked up sharply. "You want to forget me?"

"No," Rose responded, realizing the trap.

Andrew stood and crossed the deck to hold her again. She felt the warmth, and she breathed in his sunshine smell.

Rose felt her hold on the dream slipping away, and she frantically told her son she loved him until she woke up with the words still on her lips. She didn't open her eyes until the image of him had faded.

It was a little early to prepare for the race, but Rose dressed for the run and got into her car. She didn't know how she ended up at Beth's house, but she assumed it was fate when she saw the kitchen light reflecting on the lawn. Rose had almost tripped up the steps before she realized that had nothing to say. Beth saved her from formalities. She simply unlatched the door and walked down the hall. Rose followed her to the kitchen. The women stood facing each other, an island between them.

"I'm sorry," Rose began. "I was running from..." She stumbled for the words.

Beth waved her hand. "I understand your grief." She sighed. "But why didn't you respond to my messages?"

"I erased them," Rose responded honestly. "If I had heard your pain, I would have had to have dealt with my own."

Beth was crestfallen. "But not all of the messages were sad."

"I'm sorry," Rose repeated, feeling that the sentiment was not enough. "Can I be here for you now?"

In answer, Beth slid around the island. As she moved to embrace her, Rose noticed the expanding bump that pressed against her when they hugged.

"You can be here for *us*," Beth whispered.

* * *

Close to one hundred people gathered at the starting line. The clock on the town hall stood against a cornflower sky, and the minutes slowly clicked by.

Beth smiled and waved at Rose. "You can do it," she mouthed.

Rose hardly heard the whistle signal the start of the race. She was in the middle of the group, and it took almost half of the three-mile run for her to move around the other runners. She passed a few people she recognized from her cancer counseling sessions, and she waved at them. They returned her gesture with polite indifference. They had to put all of their effort into pacing themselves in the early morning sun.

Rose reached the YMCA, and she took a deep breath. Andrew had loved swimming there in the winters when he was young.

"Now you'll have someone else to take to the pool," she imagined him saying.

She whisked around the corner, the fresh breeze sending sunshine and freshly cut grass into her senses. The schools loomed in front of her. Andrew had taken Beth to his first school dance at the middle school. Rose still had the picture from the event on her mantle. She challenged herself to run faster, but not before she saw the high school's greenhouse. How many hours had she spent helping Andrew sell the produce that he and his classmates had yielded? Tears threatened to overtake her, so she stopped at a water stand the town had set up in the high school's front parking lot.

Bridget greeted her. "Are you okay, Rosie?" she asked, noticing Rose's emotions and mistaking them for physical pain.

"Definitely," Rose lied. "I have allergies."

Rose pushed herself to quicken her pace. She rounded the loop and prepared to face the same buildings again. This time, it was different. Rose recalled laughing with Andrew and his friends when they found a baby skunk in their greenhouse. It had wondered inside after someone had forgotten to close the flap. She had helped a dozen teenagers chase down the intruder before they were sprayed.

The YMCA moved past Rose in a blur, but not before she remembered when the facility had honored Andrew. He had never been a lifeguard, but he had rescued a little girl who had swam too far into the deep end. He hadn't wanted the accolades, but Rose had told him that it was important to the little girl. Andrew had accepted the certificate and had paid for swimming lessons for the girl with his own money.

The number of people running in front of Rose dwindled. She assumed someone had already won the race, but then she spoke with one of the women who was in the lead with her. She was surprised to learn that she was in the top five. Rose felt guilty for passing the remaining people. She recognized two of them from her breast cancer group, and one young man was running in honor of his father, who had passed away from lung cancer.

Rose's trek from cancer diagnosis to remission had been difficult, but it had paled in comparison to her journey through grief. Her son's loss had affected her so deeply that Rose had never thought she could recover. But there was a new voyage ahead of her. Beth's pregnancy represented the life she had been granted by God and the hope she had for the future.

The finish line was at the town hall, where the race had started. Beth was still waiting for her, and when she saw Rose in the lead, she jumped as high as her pregnant belly allowed her to and cheered. The roar of the crowd bounced off the mountains and echoed through the valley.

Rose was unconcerned about the cheers that surrounded her. In that moment, she felt her son was with her. She could almost see Andrew at the finish line, cheering alongside his wife.

"You made it happen," she heard him say.

Rose crossed the finish line and began the next lap of her life as a cancer survivor and a grandmother.

Red Snow

Linda Hudson Hoagland

The first major snowfall of the season had finally arrived. When the worst of it let up, I bundled up, pulled on my warmest boots, and ventured into the whiteness of the backyard. I was admiring gently falling flakes when I spotted something red among the drifts. The pristine beauty of the white snow was being marred or adorned, depending on which way I looked at it, by a bright red blanket near my outbuilding, which was positioned at the edge of my property. The redness looked bright, like freshly flowing blood. I shook my head side-to-side, trying to remove that image from my mind. The red snow bothered me. I had to find out why it was there.

Even though the thick, white blanket of snow was beautiful, it was difficult to trudge through. The drifts were almost impossible to navigate with my short legs. I wasn't complaining, though, because I truly loved the mountains of southwest Virginia and my tiny town of Stillwell. I pushed myself forward, lifting my legs as high as I could so I could step instead of shoving the snow. The high-stepping tired me out, but I had to find the reason for the red. I had forgotten how far my backdoor was from the outbuilding. Maybe it was just my age of seventy-one that was complaining about the distance.

I reached the red.

"My gosh, there is a person lying on the ground," I mumbled excitedly.

I reached in the pocket that usually held my cell phone, only to find that it wasn't there. I felt around in all of my pockets and could not find it. I hoped that I hadn't dropped it into the deep snow, but that didn't matter. I had to call 9-1-1.

I tried to hurry back to my house, but my old legs were moving too slowly. "Hurry, hurry, Annie," I told myself as I shoved through the snow. High-stepping would have taken too long.

When I arrived at my backdoor, I saw that the cell phone was perched on top of the small snow drift that had piled up on the back porch. I grabbed it and went inside my house to make the 9-1-1 call. When the operator answered, I asked for Barry, the chief of police and my friend.

Barry must have been standing directly behind the operator, because he answered right away. "What's wrong, Annie?" he asked.

"There's a dead man lying in the snow behind my house," I said excitedly.

"Who is it?" snapped Barry.

"I don't know. He is facedown, and I was afraid to move him to see his features," I explained.

"Are you sure he is dead?" asked Barry.

"He wasn't breathing, at least not that I could see, and there is blood covering the snow like a red blanket. I'm pretty sure he is dead," I said sadly.

"Okay, I'll be there as soon as I can," said Barry.

After we hung up, I wasn't sure what I should do. It was too cold to go outside and stand next to the body. But what if something happened? I reasoned that nothing could happen because he was dead. So I stayed inside my house because it was warm and I didn't have to see the red snow.

About fifteen minutes had passed when I heard a pounding at my front door. Expecting it to be Barry, I jerked it open without checking to see who it was. My mistake. It wasn't Barry. A big, burly man dressed in all black pushed me aside and walked inside my house, leading me to my living room. He was wearing a knitted mask over his face.

"What do you want?" I asked as I tried to be brave and forceful.

He grunted at me and motioned for me to take a seat on the sofa.

"Who are you?" I exclaimed.

He walked to the front door and began to lock each lock. I started to rise from the sofa, but he waved a gun at me that I hadn't seen when he had pushed me aside to enter my house. My mouth dropped open in surprise, and my bravery evaporated.

"What do you want?" I asked again, but this time my voice was meek, and my fear was growing by leaps and bounds.

"The man out back. Did you see what happened to him?" he snarled through the mouth opening on the mask.

"No. I don't know who he is, and I didn't see how he was killed," I stammered.

"Do you know who did it?" he snapped.

"No. I told you I didn't," I said softly. "I did walk out there to find out what all the red was in the snow, but he was already dead. Do you know him?"

"Yeah, he's my brother," he said gruffly.

"Your real blood brother or your friend brother?" I asked.

"Does it matter?" he snapped.

"No, not really. I'm sorry for your loss," I said sincerely.

He grunted again. "Did you call the cops?" he asked as he looked at the street through my front window.

"Yes, I did. I called them before you arrived here, I guess," I said as I prepared to be shot for doing such a stupid thing.

"You sit right there, and I will leave before the cops get here.

You have to stay put, or I'll have to shoot you," he said angrily. Then he was gone.

I had really thought I was a dead woman, but he hadn't been out to commit murder, I guessed.

I locked my front door and walked to the back to see if the police had arrived. No, no one was there. I started to call Barry again, but there was a knock at my door. I could see the blue lights flashing out front, so I knew it was Barry this time.

"Annie, we are going to be out behind your house for a good while. The ambulance has to get through here to get the body checked out. Is that all right with you?" asked Barry when she opened the door.

"Sure. I'll be glad when you get him out of here. When you get finished with the man that caused the red snow..." I trailed off.

"What's wrong, Annie?" he asked, concern in his voice.

"I'll tell you later. Go ahead and get your job done out back," I answered.

"You're sure?"

"Yes. Go on, Barry."

As soon as he was away from the door, I locked it. Never again would I open it without checking to see who was standing on the other side.

I watched through my window in the kitchen as they worked at the crime scene. It was several hours before they finally cleared out.

Barry came knocking at my door. "What's wrong, Annie?" he asked. He seemed to be asking me that question quite often.

"Just before you arrived, the brother of the dead man was in here, and he had a gun pointed at me," I said.

"He what?" asked a startled Barry.

"He said the dead man outside was his brother. When I asked if it was by blood or friendship, he asked me if it mattered. I believe it was his real brother because he was awfully upset," I explained.

"Did he tell you his name?" asked Barry.

"No, and he didn't remove the knitted mask that covered his face," I said.

"Oh my gosh, are you all right?" he asked.

"Yes, I guess so. I'm talking to you right now, and I was afraid that was never going to happen again," I said with a sigh.

"He didn't hurt you, did he?"

"No, but he really scared me. He wanted to make sure he left here before your guys got here. My guess is that the dead man is wanted for something."

"We couldn't find any identification on the body, so we will have to run his fingerprints and hope we can find out who he is," explained Barry.

"Will you let me know what you find out?" I asked.

"Call me in a couple of days. I'll let you know. Are you sure you are okay after your fright?" Barry asked.

"Yep, I'm fine. You can't keep this old girl down," I said as I tried to hold a broad smile in place on my aged face.

I was not all right, but I didn't want Barry to know it. That visit from the masked man had shaken me up more than I cared to admit, especially to Barry. If I showed that much agitation in front of him, he might not let me help him when I could.

It seemed that trouble knocked at my door as an uninvited guest quite often. Of course, I opened that door and unwittingly invited it in. That invitation always sent me off on another unplanned adventure. I never knew why trouble came to me, but I believed that it would keep happening until I was no longer on this earth.

The next couple of days were routine, and I was thankful for that. When the third day rolled around, I was out for some excitement of some kind. Because I was seventy-one, people thought I should stay home and count the days I had left. I didn't think so. I called Barry to get some information about the dead man.

"Hey, Annie, I bet you want some news," said a cheerful Barry.

"Yes, do you have any?" I asked.

"The man you found was Roy Morten, drug dealer and all-around bad guy. It seems that he had a disagreement with another drug dealer, and he was shot as a result," said Barry.

"Did he have a brother?"

"Yes, and he was the one who visited you," explained Barry. "By the way, he said he was sorry for bothering you."

"Did you arrest him?" I asked.

"No, I asked him questions about his dead brother. Do you want to press charges against him?"

"No, I don't think so," I said solemnly. "I think that would be asking for trouble on my part."

"You might be right about that," said Barry. "But you can press charges if you want to do so."

"No, no, not now, and hopefully not ever," I said. "What is the name of the living brother?"

"Arnold Morten, and don't go looking for him," said Barry in a stern tone.

"No problem. Talk to you later," I said, ending the conversation.

"Arnold Morten, you are going to hear from me," I mumbled, writing his name on a piece of paper so I wouldn't forget it.

I didn't want to ask Barry where I could find Arnold Morten. I didn't want him to know I was that curious. My source for information was the Internet. That had been where I had found most of my answers in the past, and I was sure I would be able to find something about Arnold Morten. I planted my behind on a chair in front of the eye to the technology world. I searched "Arnold Morten," along with "Stillwell, Virginia," and waited for the results. I was truly amazed by what popped up.

Reverend Arnold Morten of the United Destiny Church, located on 1880 Valleyview Street, would like to extend an invitation to the church to everyone.

I read that and thought that couldn't be the gun-toting masked man who had held me at gunpoint. So I continued searching, but I found no other Arnold Morten from Stillwell, Virginia. The screen displayed a photograph of his smiling face, which did me no good, as all I had seen was a mask.

"Reverend Morten, I will see you on Sunday," I mumbled as I closed down my computer so I could get something done around my house. I was not the world's greatest housekeeper, and I figured it was time for me to enter that competition again.

My mind kept wandering back to Reverend Morten. I could not figure out what would have possessed him to don a mask and point a gun at me.

Later, I took some time to sit a few moments, drink a cup of coffee, and read the newspaper. As usual, I checked the obituaries, and there it was.

Roy Morten

Morten died on May 25th and will be laid to rest at the Morten Family Cemetery on May 28th. Officiating will be Reverend Arnold Morten, brother of Roy, at 1:00 p.m.

I guessed he was the right Arnold Morten, but I wanted to see for myself.

On Sunday morning, I dressed and drove myself to Reverend Arnold Morten's church. There was a tall man there who was about the same size and build as my unwanted visitor. I hung back a bit to allow others to enter the church and greet the tall man by name. When most everyone had entered the church, I walked up to him, my right hand extended to shake his hand.

His face blanched, contrasting with the black suit he was wearing. "I'm so sorry," he sputtered as he grabbed my hand and covered it with both of his.

"I will forget about it if you will," I said. "I do need to ask one question."

"I'll try to answer it for you if I can," he said softly.

"Why the mask and gun? I'm a seventy-one-year-old widow who has lived my life as legally as I can."

"I was told that the man who was gunning for my brother lived in your neighborhood. I was looking for his killer, and obviously it wasn't you. The chief of police told me they arrested the shooter. Again, I am so sorry," he said as he hugged me.

I believed him, and I forgave him. I also found a new church to attend.

The Sixth April

Lori Byington

In the early spring of 1866, rain pitter-pattered on the old tin roof, and the smell of wet peat crept through a small, jagged crack in the window of the second-story master bedroom. A faint roll of thunder moved like waves, heading in from the ocean, down into the valley, and across the gray, dreary sky. A louder barrage of thunder sounded like a cannon blast, causing Myrtle to awake with a start.

"Lord God, tomatoes!" exclaimed Myrtle. "What was that racket?"

Instinctively, she looked to the corner for her Tennessee Soddy rifle, which she kept nearby in case someone tried to break in. Once the cobwebs were gone from her head, Myrtle realized a spring rainstorm had engulfed Paradise Valley. She breathed deeply in an attempt to clear her head and then noticed the crack in her bedside window.

"When Tal gets home, that windowpane is the first thing we need to fix," Myrtle said out loud.

She glanced around the cozy bedroom, taking in the early morning scene outside her windows, and decided she needed to get up.

Spring was Myrtle's favorite time of year, and the onslaught of mid-April rains were calming at best, and at worst they were a reminder of men in dark-blue uniforms who brandished Henry rifles and shot randomly in the air as if they were trying to make themselves more manly. This new April was the sixth since the start of the War Between the States, and all seemed quiet in the Paradise area for the most part.

As Myrtle got out of her full-size, store-bought brass bed, she glanced over at the other side, where she had been dreamily sleeping. Her cat, Blue, met her gaze and yawned. A pang hit her heart like the bolt of lightning that flashed outside her windows. She missed Tal—short for Talmadge—like the dickens and wondered for the thousandth time why he had not gotten home yet.

Myrtle knew Tal had been part of the "East Tennesseans" calvary, which was under the leadership of Brigadier-General John C. Vaughn. In fall of 1864, the regiment, as a whole, had moved back into East Tennessee from the Shenandoah area, and word down the pike was that they had helped the regiment of John C. Breckinridge capture the town of Bull's Gap. Later, in December of 1864, Myrtle received a message saying that Vaughn's men had actually been overcome back in October by General A.C. Gillem's men at Morristown, and many men had died and were wounded. After the post, a worried Myrtle had heard neither hide nor hair from Tal, nor had she heard from anyone he might have been with in the doomed calvary. Then, at the end of April in 1865, not long after the end of the war, she had received a simple, curt Western Union telegram:

Safe. Stop. Home soon. Stop. End message.

The telegram was tucked safely in her bedside table drawer, and she now pulled out the single drawer so she could gently finger the well-read piece of yellow paper. Myrtle came short of crying again, stopping herself before a tear could fall.

"No! I have to milk Elsie and feed Clara, the other hens, and Seymore. For heavens' sake, the kids can't do this on their own," she said aloud.

The only audience to her conversation was the steel-blue cat, aptly named Blue, who purred lazily on the other side of the bed. He yawned again, rolled over, and went back to sleep, his head buried in his paws.

Myrtle quickly changed from her warm, comfortable sleep attire into her daily "work" clothes. As she hung up her housecoat, she gazed at the lovely white material. Pale powder-blue flowers were embroidered in random spots on the collar. Her mother had made the coat for her wedding to Tal. Myrtle got a tight feeling in her throat and began to tear up again, but a loud bellow from the barn behind the house shocked her from her reverie.

"I guess Elsie is ready to be milked!" she said, nodding to the cat, who had awakened at the sound of the cow's impatience.

Myrtle slid into her heavy, gray wool overcoat and plopped her wide-brimmed straw hat onto her head. She tied the black ribbons tightly under her chin and silently hoped the rain would be held at bay, at least until she got to the barn. Then she slipped on her already-laced leather boots and made her way to the kitchen door. When she opened the door, a gust of mean April wind slammed into her and caught her off guard. She was forced backward awkwardly, and she ended up tripping over Blue, who had followed closely at her heels, hoping to lap up stray milk from Elsie. Unfortunately, Myrtle could not catch herself, and she unceremoniously floundered, landing with a loud "splat" in a brand-new mud puddle that had pooled in front of the door.

"Oh, dang it!" she yelled to the wind and Blue. "Lord God, tomatoes!"

Myrtle *actually* began to cry as the frigid April rain pelted her straw hat and cold drops ran down her nose. She sniffed once, then sniffed again harder, and then she put her hands down so she could attempt to get up. Unexpectedly, she found muddy water instead of a solid place from which to push off. The sudden splash sent East Tennessee mud into her face, and East Tennessee mud is like no other mud. When the mixture of orange-red clay and fertile brown dirt got wet, a bricklayer could use the gunk to build a sturdy house. Myrtle huffed loudly, glared angrily at the cat, and yelled, "Ugggg!" to the sky. She tried to get up again and managed to get herself upright. She slung her hands to relieve them from the mud, wiped her face with the ribbon from her hat, and stormed off to the barn so she could tend to Elsie and feed Clara—the main Wyandotte chicken—the other hens, and Seymore, the lone rooster of the henhouse.

Maybe the hens will have laid eggs already, Myrtle hoped. The thought put a crooked smile on her slightly muddy face.

She then heard a faint "meow" and glanced back to find Blue, who, oblivious to the mayhem he had recently caused, followed along and still anticipated spilled milk.

Around eleven o'clock, after the chores had been completed, Elsie happily munched on her hay, and the chickens scratched their hearts out. Myrtle felt a growl in her stomach. "I guess I need to eat something," she said to Blue, who was cleaning his face. He had enjoyed a stray spray of Elsie's milk. "I know you have a full belly! Now, what do I want to eat?"

Myrtle opened the barn door a stitch to make sure she would not be blown over again. She was greeted by a light mist of rain. The puffy clouds seemed to be less angry than they had been that morning. Thunder still pealed in the distance, but the deep rumbles were not as frequent. As she walked through the weathered, faded red barn door, the sun attempted to peep out from behind cumulus mounds. She glanced up and shielded her eyes with her right hand while she latched the door with her left. Sure enough, the storm was breaking, and a beautiful, full rainbow was hanging just to the east.

"Oh, what a glorious omen!" Myrtle gasped. "Maybe that is a sign Tal will be home soon," she wished out loud.

Blue meowed as if to give his two cents on the likelihood of a tall man sauntering down the driveway in the early afternoon.

Myrtle walked back toward the house she and Tal had built not long after the King plantation area had been developed. They had bought five acres on the outskirts of Paradise, Tennessee, a new city developed by a Mr. Anderson. The town was actually a stone's throw away from the Virginia state line. Myrtle and Tal's white house had royal-blue shutters and had been completed about two years before the war began, so when Tal had left to join the Confederate calvary, Myrtle had already been keeping house, and sometimes she helped with the chores with the animals. Before Tal had left for the Depot in Goodson, Virginia, he had taught Myrtle how to shoot the Tennessee Soddy. She had pretty good aim and could usually hit the tin can or whatever target Tal had found to use at the time.

When Myrtle was just about to her royal-blue front door, she noticed that the air smelled fresher. The noon sun was nearly uncovered, and all sorts of flowers had sprouted up all of a sudden. Pink crocuses, purple tulips, yellow Johnny quills, and wild onions looked like they were dancing a quadrille to the tune of the music of spring.

"Well, where did you all come from?" Myrtle asked the group.

Seeming to answer, the Johnny quills nodded their heads in unison, nudged by the breeze.

With no warning, Blue shot past Myrtle, yowling and hissing to beat the band. He ducked behind the white cane rocking chair on the front porch and glared at something behind Myrle.

"What in the world?" Myrtle yelled to the cat. "What are you doin'?"

Right as she finished her question, she heard a twig snap behind her. The sound was familiar and one she knew well. Many times, she and Tal had walked around their property to find the exact markers that showed their property lines. Many lines were set with a stake and colored ribbon. One time, they had discovered that their lines were set by a simple mark on an oak tree. She heard in her head the crisp snapping sound of a branch or twig. She, herself, had made that sound while she and Tal had made their way to claim their land. But today, she had not seen or heard anything or anyone on her walk back to the house. She had been appreciating the flora and not really paying attention.

Hairs on the back of Myrtle's neck prickled. She stiffened, and her heart beat like the drum of Isaac Woolwine. Strangely, at this moment, she remembered the youngster from Paradise who had gone to do what he could, at the tender age of sixteen, for the Confederacy. Panic rose like a knife in Myrle's throat, and she tried to think of a plan. She did not know who or what was behind her, but if Blue did not like the creature, then she knew he, or it, was not welcome.

Why did I not move my Soddy downstairs this morning! Myrtle thought to herself. *Oh, Tal will have a hissy fit over this one! I know better!*

A soft "ahem" came from behind her. She stood frozen while her eyes darted left and right. She tried to see if she could somehow catch a side glimpse of the man. The voice was clearly a male's.

"My husband will be home directly," Myrtle squeaked out. "He just went to town to get some things."

She turned slightly to her right, peeped over her shoulder, and slowly turned around completely, trying not to appear scared. Her eyes beheld a wet, disheveled, bone-thin, scraggly, bearded semblance of a man. He couldn't have been more than twenty years old, and he wore the dark blue of the Union, but the once-pristine uniform had seen much better days. The color had faded from hours in the sun. There were holes at the elbows and at the knees, some brass buttons were clearly missing, and epaulettes were long gone. Myrtle stood upright to appear taller and looked the youngster in the eyes. The young man returned the gaze but quickly lowered his sad brown eyes, cleared his throat again, and hesitated for an instant. He shuffled his feet nervously, and Myrtle noticed that his chalked boots were also pocked with holes. The fellow looked like he hadn't eaten in a month of Sundays.

"Howdy, ma'am. I didn't mean to startle ye. I saw ye out and thought maybe you could spare a biscuit and drink of water?" he asked timidly. He cautiously glanced up, hopeful.

Myrtle wiped her hands on her wool coat, took a breath in, and let it out slowly through pursed lips. Her thoughts raced. She wasn't sure she had heard him correctly, but she thought he had asked for food and water.

She breathed in again and said, as calmly as she could, "Well, I have some biscuits and a piece of country ham left over from breakfast. You can drink all you want from the spigot on the side of the house." She nodded to her right in an attempt to point to the spigot without taking her eyes off the lad. She was sure he could hear her heart thumping like Woolwine's drum.

The youngster seemed to lighten a bit. "I'd be much obliged, ma'am. I ain't had nothin' to eat in three days. I'm worn out, and I am mightily parched, too," he responded with a slight grin.

"You can get your water while I go in to get the ham and biscuits," Myrtle told him, almost motherly.

The young soldier nodded and tipped his dusty blue cap.

Myrtle watched the boy walk toward the spigot, which was on the barn side of the house. She quickly opened the door, and Blue shot in like he had been scalded. Once in the house, Myrtle locked the door and ran upstairs, taking two steps at a time. She grabbed her Soddy rifle. She made sure the gun was loaded with cap and ball, grabbed the stock, and put her finger on the trigger just in case. She walked slowly back down the stairs and glanced out the living room window to see if she could see the youngster. She could only see the top of his back because he was bent down and was splashing his face and cupping his hands to drink. Myrtle let out a whoosh of breath she hadn't realized she had been holding in.

"Lord God, tomatoes!" she said to Blue. "I need to get him some food. I can tell. But I don't know how to give the ham and biscuit to him without letting go of my Soddy."

Myrtle walked to the kitchen, opened a drawer in the oak buffet, and grabbed an old, faded pink napkin to wrap the ham and biscuit in. As she walked to the table to get the leftover breakfast, a loud racket of squawking, mad crowing, and bellowing came from the barn. "What in the dickens!" she yelled, running to the front window in time to see the youngster, obviously not as tired and hungry as he pretended to be, running out the barn door. He carried an unhappy hen under each arm and was scampering like mad up the driveway, brown and white Wyandotte feathers flying out behind him. Myrtle didn't think twice. She grabbed the Soddy, opened the front door, and raised the rifle to its place. She cocked the hammer and was comforted by the solid *click*. Then she raised the muzzle, snuggled the butt of the stock into her left armpit, and began to aim at the feathers and the young man attempting to get away with his prizes.

"All right, Myrtle," she told herself. "Just squeeze..."

Booooom! The Soddy made her ears ring and knocked her back a bit, but once the smoke cleared, she could see the backside of the young soldier. He was hightailing it farther up the driveway. He had dropped both hens and was holding on to his cap with one hand so it wouldn't fly off as he bolted out of sight.

"Well, Blue, I guess I can have leftover country ham and biscuits for my lunch!" Myrtle said aloud while she let out her pent-up breath.

She wiped her forehead with the back of her still-shaking hand, set the Soddy down just inside the front door, and began to close and lock the latch. Just as the door was about to shut out the noon sun, Myrtle heard a faint *clop, clop, clop, clop, clop* coming up the driveway. "Oh geesh. Not more unwanted company!" she said out loud.

Blue looked up at her as if to agree.

Myrtle picked up her rifle again and slowly opened the door to see who was about to trespass on her property. She could make out a man on a bay horse, but she couldn't make out his face. As horse and rider got closer to the house, the bay snorted, and the man took off his faded blue cap and waved at her.

"Haloooo, house!" he yelled. "Haloooooo!"

Myrtle's heart stopped. She dropped the rifle where she stood, stepped on Blue's tail, raised her hand to her mouth in disbelief, and felt the sting of tears as she ran toward the man riding horseback. She knew her husband's voice even though she could not make out the dear face that was covered by an unkept beard.

"Tal! Tal! Oh, Tal! You're home!" Myrtle yelled. She couldn't control her crying, but she didn't care.

Tal reined in his bay and jumped down from the saddle, both feet landing at once. "Myrtle! You are a sight for sore eyes, for sure! I missed you terribly!" Tal yelled, and he grinned, his own tears streaming down his face and into his unkept beard. He ran toward Myrtle and caught her mid-stride. The two hugged with all their might and didn't let go for a very long time.

Myrtle sniffed hard and asked, "Where have you been so long?" Then she smacked Tal playfully on his left shoulder.

"Well," Tal began. "After I wrote the telegram, I got word from Brigadier-General Vaughn that General Lee had surrendered at Appomattox, but Vaughn was having none of it! He was spittin' nails and decided to gather some of his calvary and join President Jefferson Davis on his way to Georgia. We kept fighting until it became clear that surrender was the only way. That realization, on all parts, wasn't until May tenth, though. Vaughn really was brave, but enough was enough, I guess."

Myrtle hugged Tal again tightly, smiling. "Well, you are home now, and you aren't leaving again!" Myrtle warned him.

Tal grinned down at his bride, nodded in agreement, and said, "I am home." He then paused, cocked his head to the left, and asked, "By the way, why was that kid—he looked to be Union—runnin' like a madman toward town?"

Myrtle slyly looked up and shrugged her shoulders. She responded with a chuckle. "I guess he didn't want a cap and ball in his backside, *and* he decided that two old Wyandotte chickens weren't worth the trouble."

Tal just looked at her, grinned wider, and hugged her even tighter.

Bibliography

Gordon, Larry. *The Last Confederate General: John C. Vaughn and his East Tennessee Calvary.* Zenith Press, 2009.

Phillips, Bud. "History of Bristol," *Bristol, Tennessee,* 2020, www.bristoltn.org/389/History-of-Bristol.

Jerome Believed

Linda Hudson Hoagland

Every Sunday morning, Gwen liked to go for long walks on the trail behind her house. Most of the time, she would pass one or two people, and they would nod greetings or exchange a brief sentence or two about the weather. Overall, they never made an impression on her, and she never made an impression on them. At least, not until the first Monday in August, when, after a long day of inputting information on the computer, she looked up from her supper and saw the face of a man she had passed the day before on the nightly news. She turned up the volume.

"This week on All Points Bulletin, we have a man named Jerome Marsden who is wanted for questioning regarding a murder on Baptist Valley Road."

Gwen jumped up from her seat on the sofa, nearly knocking over the small table holding her supper as she went in search of paper and a pencil. She wanted to write down his name and the phone number to call in case she passed him again. She knew it was too late to call about passing him earlier in the day, as he would be long gone from the trail.

She finished her supper and headed for her computer so she could search for Jerome Marsden and the story behind the murder. It was like the plot of a fiction novel was running helter-skelter through his life. Various websites told his story.

Jerome Marsden, 45, is a man of means due to a family inheritance. Formerly, he was a pharmacist at the local pharmacy. He worked there for many years, but the inheritance allowed him to retire permanently. It seems that he took some of that inherited money and invested it into some disreputable forms of commerce. It is not known whether or not he knew about the kind of trouble he was headed for.

Jerome had become a friend to Marty Hairston, an enterprising young man who had his fingers in many pies. Within the deepening friendship, a trust was built up between Jerome and Marty, so much so that Jerome believed everything that Marty said. Marty talked Jerome into investing in a bar right in the middle of the downtown area. Unbeknownst to Jerome, it served as a hub for ladies and men of the evening, and it was also a place for drug distribution. He was totally shocked when the place was raided by the police. The employees and customers were handcuffed and carted off to jail. When Jerome confronted Marty about the sordid sales going on in the bar, Marty professed total innocence. Unfortunately, Jerome believed Marty's lies.

Gwen took a break from snooping on the Internet and thought about what she had read about Jerome. "Gosh, I feel so sorry for him, I think," she mumbled.

* * *

When Gwen's alarm jarred her into daytime reality, she roused herself from bed so she could go for her morning walk. Maybe I will see Jerome Madsen again, she thought as she exited her home. She started out slow, peering around bushes and checking out the walking trail, looking for the alleged murderer. But the morning was so beautiful that she momentarily forgot her quest to find Jerome.

Gwen was reaching the end of her walk when she saw him. He was just standing on the path, blocking it, so she wouldn't be able to pass him without walking through the roughage on the side of the worn trail. She slowed her pace until she was almost standing still. "What should I do?" she mumbled as she glanced behind her to see if anyone was there to help her or hurt her. "No one to help," she whispered. She continued walking toward the waiting figure.

"Ma'am," he shouted at her as she was trying to figure out what to do next.

"Should I answer?" she asked herself.

"Ma'am, please. I need to ask you a question," he said in a pleading tone.

Gwen had to stop and see what he wanted. Her curiosity was getting the best of her. "What is it you need?" she asked nervously.

"I saw you on the trail yesterday. I'm sure you have seen the news since then," he said in a loud whisper.

"Yes, I have, Mr. Marsden," she said anxiously.

"Would you be able to tell me what's happening with the murder investigation?" he asked.

"The police are looking for you. You're a murder suspect," Gwen replied. "I didn't catch the name of the person you supposedly killed."

"Marty Hairston, my business partner, and I did NOT kill him," he said sternly.

"What do you want from me?" Gwen asked suspiciously.

"Your help."

"How can I help you? For that matter, why would I help you?" Gwen asked, her voice full of sarcasm.

"I need a place to sleep. I know it would be asking an awful lot, but I have no place to go. I won't harm you in any way. I promise you that. I'm just so tired," he said, swaying a bit from fatigue.

"I'm Gwen. I don't live very far from here. Come with me, and I'll feed you so we can talk some more," said Gwen as she took his arm to give him support. She knew taking him home was a danger-ous thing to do, but she just couldn't leave him there. She would do the same for a dog or a cat that needed help.

Gwen led him to her backdoor so he would be a little more hid-den from her neighbors' prying eyes. Inside, she led him to a seat. "Jerome, sit down right there. I'll get you a cup of coffee to drink for now. I'm going to go take a shower and get ready to go to the store. Before I leave, I'll get you something to eat. You can take a shower and get some rest in the guest room. If you want to wash your clothes while I'm gone, you can wear my husband's robe until your clothes are ready. Is that okay?" She filled a coffee cup and placed the cream and sugar in front of him.

"Thank you, thank you," he said as he wrapped his hands around the warm cup.

Gwen hurried through her morning routine so she could get back to the kitchen and make Jerome some breakfast. More impor-tantly, she needed to talk with him and find out what he thought she could do to help him.

"I have eggs, bacon, potatoes, and cereal. What do you want to eat?" Gwen asked as she entered the kitchen.

Jerome looked up at her and shrugged.

"What does that mean?" Gwen asked impatiently.

"Anything. I'll eat anything you have. I am so hungry," he said with a smile.

"Big breakfast coming up. You can have a bowl of cereal while I make the rest of it," Gwen said with a smile. It felt good to cook for a man. Her husband had been dead for ten years, and she truly missed that morning chore.

He devoured a bowl of corn flakes while she finished cooking the hot food. He seemed so hungry that she didn't want him to stop eating to answer her questions.

After his plate was clean, Gwen started. "Tell me what you think happened to Marty Hairston."

"I think one of the drug dealers got him," he said solemnly.

"What drug dealers? Do you do drugs?" Gwen snapped.

"It's a long story," he mumbled.

"I've got plenty of time," she replied.

"I thought you were going somewhere," Jerome said.

"That can wait. Now, tell me about your drug dealers."

"They aren't my drug dealers. As a matter of fact, I think Marty Hairston was in cahoots with them."

"Why did you partner up with him?" Gwen asked.

"He sold me on the idea of opening a bar up in the middle of town. That was a good thing, but I had no idea it was going to be a drug depot. When I questioned him about it after the police raided the place and took everyone off to jail, he got upset with me, and I thought he was going to slug me at the time. I wasn't there when the raid took place, but I had to go to court because I was one of the owners."

"What happened at court?"

"I told the judge the truth. I had no idea that drugs were being sold there. It was an investment on my part, and I didn't spend much time there. He let me off with a much smaller fine than Marty. I guess that really made him mad at me. But I swear I didn't kill him. I may have wanted to, but I didn't," said Jerome.

"Who do you think did it?" Gwen asked.

"There is this one guy whose name I have heard mentioned a lot," he said thoughtfully.

"Who is it?" Gwen asked.

"Vincent Deel."

"Do you know anything about him other than his name?" Gwen probed.

"He is shady. At least, that's what I've been told. And he was a good friend of Marty's," he said.

"Why would he want to kill his friend?" Gwen asked.

"My guess would be money," said Jerome.

"How are you going to prove it? By the way, how did Marty die?" asked Gwen.

"I think he was shot, but I really don't know for sure," said Jerome.

"I think that right now, we are going to have to find out how he was killed. I'm going to go to the grocery store, and while I'm there, I will pick up a couple of newspapers. Maybe we can find some answers printed in black and white. While I'm gone, you can get cleaned up and take a nap if you want to do that."

"Gwen, thank you so much for helping me. I will make sure you won't regret it," Jerome said with a sincere smile.

"We'll see if I do any good at finding some information."

Gwen went outside, climbed into her car, and drove to the grocery store. Her mind whirled around as she tried to understand what she was doing. She didn't know this man, but he needed help. She believed him when he said that he didn't kill Marty Hairston. He really was in a lot of trouble, and she would be, too, if they found him hiding in her house.

When she got to the store, she hurried and grabbed what she thought she needed. She spotted the newspapers and picked up the current editions from three different locations. After she left and loaded the groceries into her car, all she wanted to do was look at those newspapers. But no. She would wait until she returned home so Jerome could see them, too.

Because she was doing something illegal by harboring Jerome in her home, she was becoming a bit paranoid. She noticed police cars everywhere and was afraid they were after her. "Stop it," she told herself as she tried to shake the paranoia from her mind.

When Gwen got home, Jerome appeared at the backdoor to help with the grocery bags.

"Don't come out here. I will bring them to you, and you can place them on the kitchen table. I don't want anyone to spot you and come calling to find out who the man in my house is," Gwen explained.

"I thought you had a husband. You told me I could wear some of his clothes while I was washing mine," Jerome said.

"I did have a husband ten years ago, but he died. I've never moved his clothes out of the house. You should be glad I didn't, don't you think?" Gwen said with a smile.

"I'm sorry your husband passed away, but I'm glad I found you," said Jerome.

Gwen smiled and started putting the groceries where they belonged. When she was done, she pulled out the newspapers and spread them on the table so they could both look at them.

"There is something in this one," said Gwen as she pointed to the front page of the local paper.

Jerome glanced at the print and said, "He was stabbed, not shot."

"Over in this one, it says they have a suspect in custody," added Gwen.

"Really? Who?" asked Jerome.

"It's the man you thought might have done it. Vincent Deel," answered Gwen.

"Well, that means I'm not being chased down by the police anymore. I can go home," Jerome said, sighing with relief.

"I guess so," said Gwen.

"Can you drive me to my house?" asked Jerome.

"Sure, but let's have lunch first," she answered.

Gwen was almost sorry that her mystery had ended so soon. It had been a pleasure to spend some time with Jerome.

After eating soup and sandwiches, they headed for Gwen's car.

"Where to?" she asked.

He told her his address and directed her to his home. When they arrived, he asked her to come inside.

"No, I don't think so," she answered demurely.

"In that case, may I have the honor of taking you to dinner this evening?" he asked.

Gwen thought about it for a moment and replied, "I would love to go to dinner with you. How should I dress?"

"It's a fancy place, but it's up to you," he replied.

That date led to another and another. At the age of seventy, Gwen had thought she would never fall in love again, but she was wrong. Life was getting better. Seventy wasn't so bad after all.

Where You Are

Rebecca Williams Spindler

Her acceptance letter sits on the kitchen table. My baby girl received a four-year scholarship to Vanderbilt University. Originally, my Natalie had had her sights set on becoming the world's best music teacher. And she would have been an amazing teacher. But we lost our man of the house to the silent killer: coronavirus. Holsten was our rock, our tireless guide, my husband of twenty-six years and her daddy for eighteen. Natalie—"Nat" now—has her sights on becoming a nurse. My Nat is a remarkable young woman who has never backed away from a challenge. Instead, she steps up and puts her hard-earned skills to work. Holsten used to say she got her gumption from me.

The loss of Holsten is still a fresh wound several months later. I crawl into bed at night and crawl back out after Nat falls asleep. I creep into the living room and sleep in his easy chair. Unlike our bed, his chair still holds his scent. I need that to find any sense of rest. With our hound, Thunder, at my feet and his wedding ring around my thumb, I drift off to the ticking of the wall clock.

McCauley's rooster wakes me at 6:00 a.m. That's my signal to fold up the lap quilt, rise from the chair, and start the coffee. Nat drinks coffee these days. I'm not sure if she needs the caffeine or if she just needs to hold her daddy's mug in her hands each morning. Sometimes I can hear her crying in the shower. My heart breaks a thousand times more knowing how much she misses him.

Her hair up in a dampened bun, Nat says, "I'm taking Daddy's truck to school."

Normally, I'd bicker with her. She has her own little Nissan, a car Holsten bought for her because of the good gas mileage. Instead, I say, "That's fine, sweet pea. Drive careful. Looks like rain."

"Rained last night, Mama. It's gonna clear up today," Nat answers.

Clarity. That's something I've been lacking with the absence of my husband. I shuffle behind Nat, scrounging for anything to hand her for breakfast. I find a Moon Pie. Nat shakes her head at me, not in a scolding manner, but in worry. I get a kiss to my cheek, and out she goes.

After she leaves for school, that's when I spiral. I talk, weep, and scream at his groom portrait. What a handsome man I married. My God, he was stunning, and even more extraordinary was that that gift of a man was mine. My life is shattered without him. It's such a strange feeling to know he'll never walk back through that front door. Never. Ever. Ever. We were a team. After our wedding day, we did everything together, even the little boring things like grocery shopping, laundry, cooking, washing dishes, and walking the dog. We also did the important things together: paying bills, mailing Christmas cards, attending Nat's school concerts, dancing at weddings, and holding hands at funerals.

Funerals. There was no funeral for the light of my life. Reverend Thomas met Nat and I at the funeral home and gave a blessing as the funeral director handed over his ashes to me. Holsten is in a black ceramic box that Nat and I chose for him. He's placed in the glass hutch next to our wedding chalices.

There's a *tap, tap, tap* at the kitchen backdoor. I can tell by the gentle peck that it's Gracie McCauley. She's been our neighbor for fourteen years. Actually, Gracie's parents are the original owners of the land in the basin of Nolan holler, where a cluster of homes was built. Her family's farmhouse looks out of place in the center of our little neighborhood, but it has also been a symbol of hope in the days of the past. Gracie lost her husband, Edmund, ten years ago. That's when Holsten invited her into our family fold. She's been a surrogate granny to Nat ever since.

I open the door, and in steps Gracie, a knitted shawl around her shoulders and a warm, fresh quiche in her hands. The smell makes my mouth water, and my eyes well up in gratitude. Lately, I've only been inspired to make quick oats for Nat and me. Well, I make anything labeled "quick" these days.

"This smells divine, Gracie. Thank you."

"Eh, honey, I've got plenty of eggs. What else am I gonna do?"

She's right. Gracie's chickens have overpopulated the coop and roam the neighborhood in free range. Thunder does his best to round them up each evening, though I can tell by the beastly look in those canine eyes that he'd rather sink his teeth into a clucky or two!

"This here the letter?" Gracie finds the Vanderbilt letter.

"I should be so happy, but I'm crushed. My girl is moving on."

"Dare I say, it's a mother's job to move the children on."

Gracie knows her way around my kitchen. She pulls a plate from the cupboard and a knife from the drawer. She gets to slicing into her quiche—one hearty wedge for me, and a smaller one for her. She gives me a commanding stare that directs me to a seat at my kitchen table. Gracie puts a napkin in her lap after she sits down. She takes my hand in hers, gives it a squeeze, and closes her eyes in prayer.

"Dear Lord, hear my prayer. Give this woman the strength she needs. Help her find a way to walk a path onward and to see what's beyond that she cannot see. Amen."

How peculiar. I feel a rush of warmth come over me, like the warmth I felt when I was in Holsten's embrace. The hair raises on the back of my neck. How could this old woman bring me confirmation of a love I have lost? Affirmation is exactly what I felt in that moment. For the first time in forever, my lungs expand fully as my hands and my mind steady.

Gracie releases my hand, opens her eyes, and smiles softly. "There you be."

She lifts a fork and nibbles away at the quiche. I sit there, in awe of this peacefully spirited woman. I am reminded that I could once again feel whole. Gracie's elbow gives me a nudge. Slowly, I take a fork and break into my quiche wedge. As the morsel meets my lips, I am nourished in both my body and soul.

"What you need is a good walk. Finish up, and I'll get to washing these dishes," Gracie says as she takes a good, long look around my disheveled home. "I might spend a time or two to help tidy up a bit." She glances for my approval.

I slowly nod, and my eyes avoid hers as I devour her delicious quiche.

After breakfast, I go outside, and on this quiet, crisp March morning, I sit on a stool on the back porch wearing a corduroy jacket, my mitten-covered hands stuffed in the pockets. I pull on my rubber boots as Thunder trembles in anticipation. This hound loves galivanting through the holler, his nose on a continual crusade to hunt or track a critter. Together, Thunder and I look up the mountainside. In between the clanging of dishes that Gracie is scrubbing, I hear a train in a distant valley, its haunting *hoo-hoo* whistle echoing throughout the holler. I fasten my coat and trudge up the path to the ridge. It's the same path Holsten and I walked almost every Saturday.

Sunlight breaks through the tree branches and shines on my face. I pause, drawn to the warmth. I raise my chin and close my eyes. It only lasts a moment. As a swift wind blows a cloud into the sun's path, coldness returns, and the tree branches crackle and creak.

This Appalachian mountain ridge beckons me. Wet, rotted leaves give way to my tromping feet. With the tethered hound at my side, we ascend the trail. My breath and Thunder's are in sync. Inhaling and exhaling, we move up the steep grade step-by-step.

Spring is slow arriving to the holler this year. Only a few sparse wild daffodils brave the moist, chilled earth, along with a few redbud trees. New leaves are tiny greenlings clinging desperately to the swaying trees, their growth stunted by yet another snowfall the week before. Mother Nature's paintbrush is saturated. Instead of yellows, whites, and pinks from the daffodils, magnolias, and tulips, the landscape is awash with browns, grays, and greens. Springtime was Holsten's favorite season. It thrilled him to witness the earth's rebirth, along with the scent of April's rain and the smoky mist that hovers in the holler.

At long last, I reach the crest of the mountain. I revel as I take in the surrounding range. The only sound is the swish of brush as Thunder tramples past. The cows that wander the mountainside pastures still have their wooly coats, and steam rises from their nostrils as they graze. These Smoky Mountains are full of majestic fortitude. Like a babe at the breast, these rolling ranges bring a much-needed sense of peace to me.

Fractured sunlight peeks again through the blanket of clouds. An undeniable beam opens a door to the heavens above. The immense brightness forces me to squint and raise a hand to my brow. I instinctively peer up.

"Is that where you are?"

As if a levee has broken, tears stream, and I already know the answer. This isn't just a walk for me; it's a chance to meet him. The heat of the penetrating sunbeam releases my ache and strife. The air is the purest I have ever breathed. A bond is renewed. Sun. Earth. Air. A feeling of oneness with love, heritage, and life now renewed.

"I will return," I say to my mountain and to my man, "and I

know you'll be here waiting for me."

In what can only be defined as a youthful stroll, Thunder and I make our way back to the house. Gracie has done her sainted work, and our house resembles the home I once knew. I throw my arms around her, and in shared tears of joy and sorrow, we hold each other. When Nat returns from school, there's a congratulatory plate of homemade oatmeal chocolate chip cookies on the table next to the framed Vanderbilt acceptance letter, and a roast is in the oven.

Like pieces of a jigsaw puzzle, moments in life can leave you scattered. If you take the time to bring those pieces together and allow others to help, with grace and love, you can fit them all back into place once more.

About the Authors

Jan Howery

"A Love of Daisies"

Jan Howery, a native of Southwest Virginia, writes with an Appalachian influence. Her many writings include "The Daisy Flower Garden," featured in the anthology *Broken Petals*, and "The Devil Behind the Barn" featured in the anthology *These Haunted Hills: A Collection of Short Stories*, "The Straight Back Chair," in *These Haunted Hills Book 2*, and "Right or Wrong," featured in *Wild Daisies*. Other writings include fashion and health columns for the Appalachian regional magazine for women, *Voice Magazine for Women*.

Linda Hudson Hoagland

"As the Crow Flies"

"Help Me"

"Red Snow"

"Jerome Believed"

Linda Hudson Hoagland, a regional writer from Tazewell, Virginia, has written many mystery novels along other works of nonfiction, including the 3 volume set of *Ellen Chronicles*, 3 collections of short writings, along with 3 volumes of poems. Short stories and poems are her favorite pastime and she has won many awards for her work.

Betty Kossick

"Charlotte's Amethyst Experience"

Betty Kossick remains a versatile freelance writer/journalist/poet with five decades of published works in newspapers and magazines. With *Scattered Flowers*, she now is a part of 87 books, three of which are her solo books. "Pleasure still comes with every assignment, idea, and publication." Her work has received awards, especially in the realm of social issues.

Rebecca Elswick

"The Fallacious Life of Sadie Pringle"

Rebecca Elswick lives in southwestern Virginia where she was born. Her fiction and nonfiction works have appeared in numerous journals, among them *Still: The Journal and Deep South*. Her award-winning novel, *Mama's Shoes* was published in 2011. Elswick has an MFA from West Virginia Wesleyan College.

Courtnee Turner Hoyle

"Fawn"
"Marathon of Hope"

Courtnee Turner Hoyle lives with her husband and children in Northeast Tennessee. She holds several degrees from East Tennessee State University, and she has written *My Brother's Keeper* and the upcoming *Pinky Swear*. Discover Courtnee's newest adventure on her website www.courtneeturnerhoyle.com, or by following her on Facebook and Instagram @pale_woods_mysteries.

Lynda A. Holmes

"FHB"

Lynda A. Holmes is a lifelong Georgia resident, retired educator, and author. Her publications include professional articles, poetry, memoirs, southern fiction, and historical fiction (*Mineral Spirits*, JCP 2015). She won the American Heritage National First Place Awards for Drama and Poetry from the National Society Daughters of the American Revolution.

Lori Byington

"The Sixth April"

Lori Byington resides in Bristol, TN with her husband and son. She is Assistant Professor of English at King University. Lori loves to snow ski and write, and has been published in previous JCP anthologies *Broken Petals, Easter Lilies, Wild Daisies, Snowy Trails,* and *These Haunted Hills Book 2.*

Rebecca Williams Spindler

"Where You Are

Rebecca Williams Spindler is a content creator, author, award-winning screenwriter and film producer. She's been a writing instructor for Madison Area Technical College and presented workshops at University of Wisconsin Writers Institute. She's also a script reader for Nashville Film Festival screenwriting competition. She's a midwestern mama with roots in Scott County, Virginia. Follow her Facebook: www.facebook.com/fansofspindlerwriting or Twitter: spindler_writer.

**Jan-Carol
Publishing, Inc**

"every story needs a book"

**LITTLE CREEK BOOKS
MOUNTAIN GIRL PRESS
EXPRESS EDITIONS
DIGISTYLE
ROSEHEART
BROKEN CROW RIDGE
FIERY NIGHT
SKIPPY CREEK**

JanCarolPublishing.com

CPSIA information can be obtained
at www.ICGtesting.com
Printed in the USA
LVHW030327250821
696016LV00001B/8